A Note from Lucy Daniels

Dear readers,

I'm so excited that Hodder Children's Books is publishing your favourite titles as Animal Ark Classics. I can't believe it's ten years since Mandy and James had their first adventure. I've written so many stories about them they feel like real friends to me now and it's been such fun thinking up new stories for them both.

I know from your letters how much you enjoy sharing their love of animals. As you can tell, I'm a huge fan of animals myself, and can't imagine a day when I will ever want to stop writing about them.

Happy reading!

Very best wishes,

Lucy

LUCY DANIELS

ANIMAL ARK
CLASSICS

PONY IN THE PORCH

**Hodder
Children's
Books**

a division of Hodder Headline Limited

Special thanks to C. J. Hall, B.Vet.Med., M.R.C.V.S.,
for reviewing the veterinary information contained in this book.

Animal Ark is a trademark of Working Partners Ltd
Copyright © Working Partners Ltd 1994
Created by Working Partners Ltd, London W6 0QT
Original series created by Ben M. Baglio
Illustrations copyright © Shelagh McNicholas 1994

First published in Great Britain in 1994 by Knight Books

This edition published in 2004 by Hodder Children's Books

The right of Lucy Daniels to be identified as the Author of
the Work has been asserted by her in accordance with the
Copyright, Designs and Patents Act 1988.

For more information on Animal Ark, please contact
www.animalark.co.uk

2 4 6 8 10 9 7 5 3

A Catalogue record for this book is available from the British Library

ISBN 0 340 87704 9

Typeset in Baskerville by Avon DataSet Ltd,
Bidford-on-Avon, Warwickshire

Printed and bound in Great Britain by
Clays Ltd, St Ives plc

The paper and board used in this paperback by Hodder Children's
Books are natural recyclable products made from wood grown in
sustainable forests. The manufacturing processes conform to the
environmental regulations of the country of origin.

Hodder Children's Books
a division of Hodder Headline Limited
338 Euston Road
London NW1 3BH

To Helen Magee

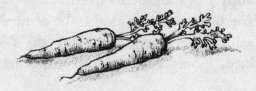

One

The little Welsh pony nibbled gently at Mandy's fingers as she fed him the last of the carrots she had brought for him. 'There, boy,' she said running her free hand down his silky neck. 'Oh, Prince, I'm going to miss you.'

'So am I,' said Mrs Jackson. 'But there's nothing else we can do now that Jane has gone to live in York. There's nobody to exercise him and ponies are expensive to keep.'

'How is Jane's nursing course going?' said Mandy. Jane was Mrs Jackson's daughter. Mrs Jackson had been a widow for five years and she and

Jane lived at Rose Cottage, just along the road from where Mandy's grandparents lived.

'Oh, Jane has always wanted to be a nurse,' Mrs Jackson said. 'She's loving it. But she's worried about Prince. I only hope we can find him a good home.'

Mandy looked round the little orchard at the back of Rose Cottage. Prince's stable was a simple lean-to shed in a sheltered corner of the orchard. It smelled of sweet grass and tangy peat moss and the air blew fresh and clean under the trees. 'He couldn't find a better home than this,' she said.

'He's always been happy here,' said Mrs Jackson. She lifted a hand and laid it on Prince's gleaming brown coat. 'Eight years we've had this pony,' she said. 'It was Jane's tenth birthday present. I remember the day Fred brought him home. You would have thought he had given Jane the moon, she was so pleased.' Mrs Jackson wiped a tear away. 'Oh, well,' she said. 'What has to be done has to be done, I suppose.'

Mandy smiled at her although she felt sad too. 'I'm sure you'll find a good home for him, Mrs Jackson.'

'I won't be sending Prince anywhere they can't keep him properly,' Mrs Jackson said. 'When I think of all the rosettes he's won at the Welford Show. He's a grand little jumper. Nearly as good as that pony of young Barry Prescott's.'

'Barry's pony is bigger than Prince,' Mandy said. Barry Prescott was the local doctor's son. He had a bay gelding called Star.

Mrs Jackson was looking at her. 'I don't suppose you would want a pony now, would you, Mandy? I know you would look after him.'

Mandy laughed. 'I've got an ark full of animals, Mrs Jackson. Mum says if we had any more we would sink. But I *will* miss him, won't I, boy?' and she buried her face in Prince's neck.

A voice called from two gardens away. It was Gran. Mandy had gone round to say goodbye to Gran and Grandad. They were going off for two weeks in the sun. She often popped in to see Prince when she was round at Lilac Cottage, and Jane had often let Mandy groom him and feed him. 'That must be Gran and Grandad leaving,' she said to Mrs Jackson.

'You get off and give them a hug before they go,' Mrs Jackson said. 'And tell them I hope they have a good time in Portugal.'

'I'll tell them,' Mandy said, giving Prince a final pat. 'See you soon,' she said to the little pony as she left. She waved as she got to the gate at the back of the orchard. Prince was cropping the grass contentedly. Yes, she would certainly miss him.

'That's us all ready,' said Gran as Mandy turned in at the back gate of Lilac Cottage. 'Now give me a hug and tell us to have a good time and see if you can get your grandad out of his vegetable garden or we'll miss our plane.'

Mandy laughed and chivvied Grandad out of his garden.

Grandad shook his head. 'It's the leeks,' he said. 'I want them perfect for the Welford Show.'

Gran tutted. 'Now you know Walter Pickard is going to look after them for you,' she said. 'They'll still be there in two weeks' time.'

Mandy's father appeared at the back door of the cottage. 'Any takers for a holiday in Portugal?' he said to his parents. 'If you don't fancy it after all, Emily and I could go.' He winked at Mandy. Dad was driving Gran and Grandad to the airport.

Gran gave her son a look, 'And leave Animal Ark?' she said. 'You wouldn't stop worrying about it, Adam Hope.'

Mandy laughed as Dad bundled Gran and Grandad into the car and set off. She watched the car disappear down the lane and got on her bike to go home. She wasn't going to the airport. She had a few things to do at home, like check up on a rabbit with an infected paw and pay a visit to a puppy that had been abandoned with a broken leg. Betty Hilder had brought him in and Mandy had named him Toby. Betty ran the local animal sanctuary.

She hadn't been joking when she told Mrs Jackson they had an ark full of animals. They did — Animal Ark, where her mum and dad were vets.

Mandy whizzed down the road, long legs pedalling and thoughts of Toby and Prince filling her mind. She was sure Betty could find a home with somebody in the village for Toby — he was so cute and lovable. But she might only see Prince a few more times before he had to leave Welford.

There was a new girl in Mandy's class. She stood beside Miss Potter. She didn't look very cheerful. Mandy sighed. She was still thinking about Prince — only now she wondered where he was. She had been so busy these last two weeks she hadn't had time to go round to Rose Cottage until just a few days ago. The stable in the orchard had been empty and Mrs Jackson wasn't at home. Mandy had just stood there with the sun dappling the grass at her feet. She had stared at the empty stable for a long time, her eyes until blurred over with tears. Prince was gone.

'This is Susan Collins,' Miss Potter was saying. Miss Potter was Mandy's form teacher. She was really nice, with flyaway mouse brown hair and big spectacles. Mandy looked at Susan. She wasn't as tall as Mandy and she wasn't as thin either. Her dark hair was drawn back in a ponytail.

That made Mandy think of Prince again. It wasn't so much that he had gone away. After all she knew he was going. It was not saying goodbye properly that hurt so much. Even her mum and dad hadn't heard where Prince had gone.

'Now,' said Miss Potter, 'I need somebody to help Susan settle in. Mandy, you could do that.'

Kate and Melanie, Mandy's friends, nudged her. 'Wake up,' said Kate.

'I can find my own way round,' Susan was saying. Her voice sounded different. Not like a Yorkshire voice.

Miss Potter carried on regardless. 'Susan comes from London,' she said. 'So living in the country is going to be a big change for her.' She put Susan in the seat beside Mandy. 'But I'm sure you will all help her — especially you, Mandy.'

As Susan sat down Mandy said, 'You'll soon get

used to it. It must be hard coming to a new school.'

'I don't want to get used to it,' Susan said. 'I want to go back to London. London was much better than this.'

'Wait and see,' Mandy said encouragingly. 'You'll like it once you get to know everybody.'

Susan tossed her ponytail. 'I won't,' she said. 'I hate it. There's nothing to do.'

Mandy thought about all the things she did — especially helping out at Animal Ark. 'There's always loads to do in the country,' she said. 'You'd be surprised.'

'Like what?' said Susan.

'Well,' said Mandy, 'we've got the Welford Show on Saturday. That's terrific. There are sideshows and pet shows and a gymkhana and . . .'

'A gymkhana?' said Susan. She looked thoughtful.

'You see,' said Mandy. 'You'll like living here.'

Susan scowled. 'I won't,' she said as Miss Potter started the lesson. 'And you won't make me — not you or anybody else.'

Mandy blinked. Susan sounded really determined to hate her new home. She wondered why.

By half past three that day Mandy had decided that Susan Collins was a complete pain. At lunch-time, when they were talking about where they lived, it had been the house she lived in.

'It's called The Beeches,' Susan said, her nose in the air. 'It's the new house on the Welford road. It has a veranda running all the way round the front and stables at the back and a paddock going right down to the road.'

Mandy and James passed that way every day biking to school. So that was who had moved into the big new house. 'That must be terrific,' she said.

Susan turned to her. 'It's a lot better than living in a poky little cottage,' she said. 'Imagine living in an ark. I think I'll call you Mrs Noah.'

Then at break it had been her computer. 'Have you got one, Mrs Noah?' Susan asked after spending five minutes telling Mandy everything her computer could do.

Mandy shook her head. 'No, but James has. He really likes computers.'

'James who?' said Susan.

'James Hunter,' Mandy said. 'He lives in Welford too. We cycle to school together every day.'

'Is he your boyfriend?' said Susan.

'No,' Mandy said, trying to keep her temper. 'He's just a friend.' Susan really was annoying.

All day long Susan didn't miss a chance to say how much she hated the country. But as she walked Susan to the school gate at half past three Mandy got a surprise.

'Isn't there anything you like about being here?' Mandy said.

Susan looked as if she were going to say no. Then she stopped. 'Dad bought me a pony,' she said. 'I like that.'

Mandy's eyes popped. 'A pony!' she said. 'Can you ride?'

'Of course I can ride,' said Susan. 'I learned in London. At the best riding-school, of course. I did showjumping as well.'

Mandy's eyes were shining. 'Ponies are lovely,' she said. 'You'll have great fun looking after a pony.'

Susan snorted. 'The stables looked after the ponies where I learned to ride,' she said. 'I didn't have to do a thing.'

'But didn't you want to do it yourself?' said Mandy.

'Ugh!' said Susan. 'Nasty smelly old straw and mucking out. No, thank you, Mrs Noah.'

'But if you have your own pony . . .' said Mandy.

Susan shrugged. 'The gardener looks after it,' she said.

Mandy shook her head. How could anyone have a pony and not want to look after it? That was the fun of it.

'I couldn't be bothered with all that,' Susan said. 'I just like riding. My mum is a wonderful rider.'

'Has she got a horse as well?' said Mandy.

Susan looked away. 'No,' she said. 'She lives in London. She has to. She's an actress. She's famous. She's in *Parson's Close*. She plays the vicar's wife.'

'My gran watches that on TV,' said Mandy. 'She loves it.' Then she stopped. Suddenly Susan was looking terribly unhappy. 'Is that why you want to go back to London?' said Mandy. 'Because your mum's there?'

For a moment she thought Susan was going to answer her. But Susan only laughed and said, 'Why would anybody want to stay in a stupid place like this when they could live in London? What is there to do — apart from your stupid Welford Show?'

'The Welford Show *isn't* stupid,' Mandy began.

But Susan wasn't listening. Her eyes were alight. 'Maybe if I got her interested in horses again. She used to be interested . . .'

'Hi!' James came up to them, wheeling his bike. His straight brown hair was tousled as usual and his glasses were halfway down his nose.

'This is Susan,' said Mandy. 'She's new and her dad's coming to collect her.'

'In his car,' Susan said. 'It's a Jaguar.'

'Haven't you got a bike? Why don't you cycle to school like us?' James said. 'It's good fun.'

Susan put her nose in the air. 'Of *course* I've got a bike,' she said. 'A mountain bike. And it's much better than those two.'

James looked at Mandy. 'Our bikes are OK,' he said.

Susan just smiled. 'Wait till you see my dad's car,' she said. She turned to Mandy. 'Is your dad rich?' she said.

Mandy thought of her dad. Sometimes he treated

the animals people brought to him for free. Like
Tommy Pickard's hamsters. Tommy was seven and
hadn't realised that feeding chewing-gum to
hamsters wasn't good for them. He came into
Animal Ark every day to see how they were getting
on.

'No, my dad isn't rich,' said Mandy, 'but the
animals are lovely.'

Susan looked at her. 'I suppose you talk to them,'
she said.

'Of course,' said Mandy. 'Animals like being
talked to. Don't you talk to your pony?'

Susan tossed her head. 'That's different,' she said.
'I wouldn't talk to hamsters.'

'*All* animals like being talked to,' said Mandy
firmly.

Susan just laughed. 'I don't think I'll call you Mrs
Noah any more,' she said. 'I think I'll call you
Doctor Doolittle. You talk to the animals.'

Mandy got really cross then. 'It's better than
talking to some people,' she said.

Just then a big blue Jaguar drew up outside the
school gates. There was a man in the driving seat. He
leaned over and opened the passenger door. 'Hello,'
he said. 'I see you've made friends already, Susan.'

Susan's father looked across at Mandy and James.

He was smiling. He had a nice smile but, just the same, he looked as if he was thinking about something else.

'Why don't you ask your new friends to tea?' he said to Susan. 'How about Wednesday? I'll let Mrs Taylor know.' Then he looked at his watch. 'Get in, Susan,' he said. 'I'm in a hurry. I have a meeting to go to.'

Susan tossed her hair and made a big thing of getting into the car.

'See you tomorrow,' Mandy said as the car took off in a rush.

James turned to Mandy. 'What a pain that girl is,' he said.

Mandy wheeled her bike out of the gates. 'I really tried to be friendly,' she said. 'But all she does is boast about what she's got and how rich they are.'

'Forget it,' said James. 'How are Tommy's hamsters?'

Mandy smiled and shook her head. 'Poor things,' she said. 'Dad had to snip off most of their whiskers and all the fur round their noses and paws. They were covered in the stuff. We're keeping them at the Ark for a few days just to make sure they didn't swallow any of it.'

Mandy launched into an update on all of Animal

Ark's patients. James had a Labrador retriever called Blackie and a kitten called Eric. He was always interested in hearing about animals.

By the time they got to the Fox and Goose, where the track to Animal Ark branched off, Mandy had nearly forgotten Susan. Nearly but not quite. At least she hadn't forgotten the pony. They brought their bikes to a halt.

'See you tomorrow,' said James.

'Don't forget to tell your mum you're going to tea at Susan's posh house on Wednesday,' said Mandy.

James pushed his glasses up on to the bridge of his nose and looked at her.

'You don't have to go,' he said. 'I mean, why punish yourself?'

Mandy bit her lip. 'Wouldn't you like to see the pony?' she said.

James shook his head. 'You're impossible!' he said. 'You don't even like her.'

Mandy grinned. 'I know,' she said. 'But it isn't Susan I'll be going to see − it's the pony.'

James grinned back and shook his head. 'All right,' he said. 'I give up. Count me in.'

Mandy watched him cycle off. James lived at the other end of the village. Mandy wheeled her bike up the path to the old stone cottage. The path up to the red front door ran between banks of flowers and a wooden sign saying 'Animal Ark, Veterinary Surgeon' swung in the breeze. The veterinary surgery was a modern building tacked on to the back of the cottage.

The surgery window was open. Mandy waved to Jean Knox, the receptionist, as she wheeled her bike past.

Jean waved back cheerfully, her glasses dangling on the end of their chain. 'Had a good day at school?' Jean called.

Mandy shrugged. 'It was all right,' she said.

Jean gave her a look but didn't say anything. Simon, the practice nurse, came to the window. 'Never mind,' he said. 'Everybody has a bad day sometimes. The animals are waiting for you.'

Mandy looked at the two faces. 'Oh, it wasn't so bad,' she said and Jean smiled.

It was good to be home. Gran and Grandad were due back from holiday late tonight. Maybe they would know where Prince was — and Mrs Jackson. And soon she would go round and see Toby — and find out how those hamsters of Tommy's were doing. And she would talk to them, she thought. No matter what Susan Collins said.

Two

When Mandy woke up next morning the sun was shining through her bedroom window. It was a lovely day. She lay perfectly still for a moment and looked round.

She loved her bedroom. It had a low whitewashed ceiling with dark oak beams. The walls were covered with animal posters. And Mum had let her choose her own furniture. There was a pine chest at the foot of the bed and a cupboard in the corner under the eaves. And she had a table in the window where she could sit and do her homework looking out at the garden below.

Then Mandy remembered Susan Collins and groaned as she got out of bed. 'Oh, well,' she said to a poster of a baby seal, 'at least I'm going to see the pony tomorrow.' She ran a brush through her short blonde hair.

'Mandy,' called a voice from downstairs. 'Are you up yet? Or is that a herd of elephants clumping about in your room?'

Mum. Mandy grinned, got up and opened her bedroom door. The smell of freshly made toast drifted up the stairs to her. She hung over the banister of the narrow wooden staircase. 'Morning, Mum,' she called. 'I'll be right down.'

'Don't bring the elephants,' called another voice. Her dad.

She showered and dressed in double-quick time and raced downstairs. 'Mmm,' she said as she tucked in to toast and homemade marmalade. 'This is wonderful.'

She looked up at her parents – her adopted parents, really, but it never seemed that way to Mandy. Adam and Emily Hope had adopted her when her own parents had been killed in a car crash years ago – when she was a baby. Adam Hope was dark haired and jolly and really easy-going. Emily had red curly hair and was the organiser in the family. It was funny. They were both vets but they were so different.

'Gran and Grandad got back last night,' said Mum.

Mandy spoke through a mouthful of toast. 'Did you ask them about Mrs Jackson — oh, and did they have a good holiday?'

Mrs Hope laughed. 'They had a great time and they said Mrs Jackson has gone to stay with Jane for a few weeks in York.'

'So what about Prince then?' said Mandy. 'Is he sold?'

'They don't know,' Mrs Hope said. 'They found a postcard from Mrs Jackson waiting for them when they got home. She didn't mention Prince.'

Mandy gave a deep sigh. Mum looked up. 'What's wrong?' she said.

Mandy shrugged. 'It's nothing,' she said. 'I wish I knew where Prince had gone.'

'Is that all?' said Mum.

Mandy didn't say anything. 'Come on, Mandy,' said Dad. 'If your mum thinks there's something wrong, you can bet your boots there's something wrong. Out with it.'

Mandy looked from one to the other. 'It's just this new girl at school,' she said.

'What new girl?' said Dad.

'Susan Collins,' said Mum.

Mandy looked at her. 'How do you know about her?' she said.

Mrs Hope laughed. 'From Mrs McFarlane at the post office,' she said. 'Honestly, if a mouse sneezes that woman hears about it.'

'Does this Susan have a mouse with a cold then?' said Dad.

Mrs Hope gave him a look. 'Isn't it time you went to work?' she said.

Mr Hope grinned and got up from the table. 'OK, I can take a hint,' he said as he disappeared out of the kitchen door.

'So, what's the problem with Susan Collins?' Mrs Hope asked.

Mandy looked at her mum. She had green eyes and freckles and the kind of smile that made you want to tell her everything.

'Miss Potter asked me to look after her because she's new, but she's horrible, Mum.'

Mum nodded and poured out another cup of tea for them both. 'You've only just met her,' she said.

Mandy shrugged. 'She says I'm loopy because I talk to animals. She calls me Doctor Doolittle.'

Mrs Hope was smiling.

'What are you laughing at?' said Mandy. 'It isn't funny.'

'I'm not laughing,' said her mum. 'I'm just smiling because I remember what it used to be like. And it wasn't funny for me either.'

Mandy's eyes opened wide. 'You mean people used to say things like that to you?' she said. Her mum nodded and Mandy smiled. It made her feel a lot better. 'Anyway, James and I are going to her house for tea tomorrow. Is that all right?'

Mum nodded. 'Of course it is. But why on earth are you and James going if you don't like her?'

Mandy's eyes slid away from her mother's. 'Um, well, she's got this pony . . .' she began sheepishly.

'You're a disgrace, Mandy Hope,' Mum said with a laugh.

'I don't think Susan wants us to come,' said Mandy. 'It was her dad that invited us.'

There was a sound of gravel spurting outside and a bicycle bell pinged. 'That'll be James,' Mandy said. 'I'd better go.' She got up from the table and grabbed her schoolbag. She was at the door when her mother spoke.

'Mandy,' she said.

Mandy turned. 'Mmm?' she said.

'This girl Susan,' Mrs Hope said. 'She's only just

moved here. Maybe she's lonely. There's only her and her dad at that big house and her dad is too busy working to have much time for her. He's setting up that new building project on the other side of Walton.'

Mandy nodded. 'I know. Her dad is really rich according to Susan and her mum's a famous actress.'

Mrs Hope smiled. 'She's in one of the soaps Gran watches,' she said. 'Gran wrote to her before she went away to ask her to give out the prizes at the Welford Show.'

Mandy groaned. 'Susan's bad enough as it is. Just think what she'll be like if her mum's doing the prize giving. Has she said she'll do it?'

Mrs Hope started clearing the table. 'Gran's waiting for an answer.' Gran was chairperson of the Welford Women's Institute.

Suddenly Mandy grinned. 'What about Mrs Ponsonby?' she said. 'She always does the prize giving.'

Mrs Ponsonby was a leading light in the Women's Institute. She was really bossy. She lived in creepy old Bleakfell Hall and had a fat Pekinese called Pandora.

'Let's put it this way,' said Mrs Hope. 'I wouldn't like to be the one to tell Mrs Ponsonby her services won't be required.'

Mandy shrugged. 'She deserves to be taken down a peg or two,' she said. 'And she overfeeds that poor little peke of hers dreadfully.'

The bicycle bell pinged again and Mandy jumped. 'I'd better go.'

'Now, remember,' said Mrs Hope, 'try to make friends with Susan.'

Mandy opened her mouth to protest but she changed her mind. She had to admit that it must be difficult for Susan not to have her mum around all the time. 'OK, Mum,' she said. 'I'll try, but I don't think it'll do any good.'

James popped his head round the kitchen door. 'Are you coming?' he said to Mandy. 'Hello, Mrs Hope.'

'Good morning, James,' said Mum. 'How's Eric?'

'He's a holy terror,' said James, grinning. 'He's driving my mother wild.'

'Huh,' said Mandy. 'Your mum loves that kitten.'

James grinned again. 'So does Blackie,' he said. 'Come on. If we hurry we won't be late.'

Mandy and James pedalled up the hill that led out of Welford. As they passed the church Mandy caught sight of a familiar figure in the field behind. She slowed her bike and stopped by the stone wall that ran round the field. 'Hi, Grandad,' she called excitedly. 'How was the holiday?'

Grandad looked up from a post he was hammering into the ground. 'Mandy,' he said and started to walk towards them. 'We had a great time. And best of all, my leeks survived.'

'Hi, Mr Hope,' said James. 'Getting things ready for the show?'

Grandad nodded and passed a hand over his brow. 'It's hard work for an old man like me. What we need is some young blood.'

Mandy laughed. Her grandad might be retired now but he was as fit as a fiddle — and really tanned after two weeks in the sun.

'You're young blood compared to some of us,' said a voice and old Walter Pickard appeared round the corner of the churchyard. Walter had once been the local butcher but he had been retired a long time now. He was a lot older than Mandy's grandad but he was still spry. 'How're those hamsters of our Joe's boy getting on?' he said to Mandy.

Tommy was Walter's great-grandson and the apple of his eye.

Mandy laughed. 'They're recovering,' she said. 'Dad says we'll keep them until the show — just in case.'

'What are you doing?' asked James.

Grandad laid down his mallet. 'Trying to get the jumps sorted out for the pony trials,' he said.

'Aye,' said Walter. 'We want to make sure they're suitable. We need somebody to try them out. Usually Barry Prescott does it but Star is getting over a sprained tendon and he doesn't want to risk it just yet.'

'We know somebody with a pony,' said James. 'We could ask her.'

'Susan?' said Mandy, her eyes widening.

'Bring her along on Thursday,' said Grandad. 'They should be ready by then.'

James was hanging over the wall. 'If you need help, we could come over too,' he said.

'Good for you,' said Walter. He looked at his watch. 'Mind you aren't late for school now.'

'Cripes,' said James. 'Come on, Mandy. We might just make it.'

They pedalled hard to make up for lost time and they were well out on the Walton road before they slowed down a bit. Mandy was enjoying the sun on her back and the breeze on her cheeks. Suddenly it was a lovely morning again. She said so to James and he grinned.

'Was something wrong?' he said.

Mandy made a face. 'Only Susan Collins,' she said.

'You should try to ignore her,' said James.

Mandy looked at him. 'Mum says I should try to make friends with her.

'Friends?' said James.

And Mandy laughed at the expression on his face. 'That's how I feel,' she said. 'But I'll try — for Mum's sake.'

They passed the big new house where Susan lived. It had lawns and a paddock in front and Mandy could just catch a glimpse of stables at the back. There was no pony in the paddock.

'Imagine living in that,' said James.

Mandy looked at it. 'I would rather live in our cottage than that,' she said.

'You would rather live in your cottage than anywhere else in the world,' said James.

Mandy smiled at him, 'You're right. I would.'

She pedalled faster and lifted her face to the clear country air and the sun. The fields were green with new corn and on the low hills in the distance she could see this year's lambs picking their way amongst the tussocks. Dad said it had been a good year for lambing. Mandy sometimes wished the tiny little lambs didn't grow up so quickly but Dad only laughed at her when she said that.

'Look at you,' he said. 'You wouldn't want to stay the same for ever, would you?'

But sometimes Mandy thought it would be nice to stay the same for ever — if it meant staying in Welford at Animal Ark and looking after animals. But nothing stayed the same for ever. Even the animals moved on — like Prince going to a new home. She was sure she would be happy if only she knew he was safe and well with people who would love him and look after him.

Three

They were only five minutes late and Miss Potter was really good about it when Mandy told her why. 'Tell your grandfather if he needs any help selling tickets at the gate or anything like that then I'll happily do it,' she said.

'Thanks, Miss Potter,' Mandy said. It was wonderful how people got involved in the Welford Show.

Susan and Mandy were in different sets for most subjects so they didn't see much of each other in lessons. Mandy asked her to join Melanie and Kate and herself for lunch.

'I've already found a place,' said Susan shortly. Then she turned back. 'Oh, by the way, Mrs Taylor says come at six tomorrow night.'

Mandy didn't even get a chance to ask who Mrs Taylor was.

'Don't bother about her,' said Melanie after Susan walked away.

'She's a pain,' said Kate. 'Good riddance.'

Mandy sighed. 'Maybe she's just homesick,' she said, but Kate and Melanie didn't seem to think so.

Just then Barry Prescott stopped by their table. 'That liniment your dad gave me really worked,' he said to Mandy.

Mandy smiled. 'Oh, I'm glad, I'll tell him. Will Star be all right for the show then?'

Barry nodded. 'No problem,' he said. 'We should win the jumping again.'

'Barry always wins,' said Melanie as Barry moved on.

'James is putting Blackie in for the pet show,' said Mandy. 'He's been teaching him tricks.'

'Blackie?' said Kate. 'I've seen some of Blackie's tricks.' Blackie wasn't exactly known for his obedience but James loved him anyway.

'Like the time he ran away with the hockey ball at the inter-schools final,' said Melanie.

They all giggled. 'I don't think James has been allowed to bring him to any kind of school match since,' said Mandy.

'That dog's a dangerous animal,' said Kate and they laughed.

On the way home from school Mandy saw a brown pony at the far end of The Beeches' paddock. It looked so like Prince her heart gave a lurch. Talk about wishful thinking.

'How are Blackie's tricks coming on?' she said to James to take her mind off Prince.

'I'm teaching him to fetch things,' James said.

'Is it working?' said Mandy.

James grinned. 'Not so that you'd notice. He fetches things all right. They just aren't the things you want him to fetch. You should have heard Mum the other day. Blackie came downstairs with a pillow.'

'And?' said Mandy.

'He started to chew it,' James said. 'There were feathers everywhere and Blackie chasing them. Every time he sees a feather now he goes for it. He even recognises the word because Mum was storming around the house shouting "feathers, *feathers*, FEATHERS".'

James was coming to Animal Ark as well. They drew up outside, still laughing about Blackie.

'What's got into you two?' said Jean from her desk as they passed by.

'Feathers,' they both said and she shook her head in despair at them.

Just then there was the sound of car wheels on gravel. Mandy and James turned to the door as it flew open. It was little Penny Hapwell from Twyford Farm. Her mother was carrying a small furry bundle wrapped in a towel — Cally, Penny's kitten. Blood was soaking through the towel and the kitten's eyes were closed. Mandy's heart turned over as she looked at Mrs Hapwell's shocked face.

'She isn't dead, is she?' Mandy said but, looking at the little scrap of tortoiseshell fur it was hard to believe Cally could still be alive.

At once Jean became brisk. She rang a buzzer on her desk and Simon came in immediately.

He took one look at the scene and tapped on the treatment room door. Mr Hope appeared, took in the situation at a glance and gently patted Penny's head. 'My, my,' he said, 'Cally has had an accident, has she? Well, you're not to worry, OK?'

The little girl looked up at him, her eyes big with tears. 'You'll make her better, Mr Hope, won't you?' she said. 'Mummy says you'll make her better.'

Mr Hope smiled at the little girl but Mandy saw the urgent look he gave Simon. Simon lifted the blood-soaked bundle out of Mrs Hapwell's hands and bore it off into the treatment room.

Mr Hope turned to Mandy. 'Look after Penny while I have a word with Mrs Hapwell, will you?'

Mandy nodded. She couldn't trust herself to speak. She could see how serious the situation was.

Jean looked at Mandy and lowered her voice. 'Now you go and get that little girl some milk and biscuits and don't go upsetting yourself,' she said. 'You know if anybody can save that little kitten your dad can.'

Mandy nodded dumbly. She felt sick to the pit of her stomach. Poor little kitten. Poor Penny. Mandy remembered well the little girl bringing her kitten in for its injections not long after it was born.

'Come on, Mandy,' said James. 'We'll hear soon enough.'

Mandy nodded. She was at the connecting door between the house and the surgery when she said to Jean. 'Where's Mum?'

'Over at Baildon,' Jean said. 'Nothing terrible. Just a horse needing a once-over before he's sold.'

Mandy nodded again and let James push her gently through the door into the house. She poured milk and put out a plate of biscuits for Penny, who couldn't eat anything. All Mandy could think of was what was going on next door.

'Why don't we take Penny through and show her the animals in the residential unit?' James said.

Mandy nodded. 'Would you like that, Penny?'

The little girl thought for a moment. 'Has your daddy made Cally better yet?' she said.

Mandy bit her lip, 'Not yet,' she said. 'But he will.'

Penny nodded solemnly. 'I know,' she said. 'Mummy says so.'

They were in the unit when Mrs Hapwell came in. 'Jean and I think it's best if we go home,' she said. 'She'll ring when she's got news.'

'Is it going well?' Mandy said.

Mrs Hapwell shrugged. 'I was only in there long enough to tell him what happened. I've been talking to Jean.' She looked at Penny. 'Come on, love,' she said. 'Let's go home.'

'I want Cally,' said Penny, tears threatening once more.

Mrs Hapwell bent down and gave her a hug. 'We have to leave Cally here for a little while,' she

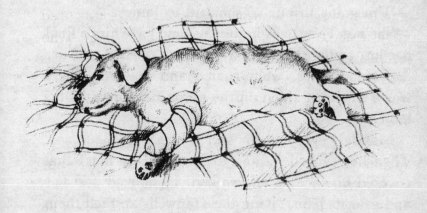

said. 'Until she gets better.'

Penny nodded. 'Just till she gets better,' she said.

Mrs Hapwell looked at Mandy over her daughter's head and Mandy knew at once why she was taking her home. If Cally didn't get better it would be easier if Penny was at home.

After they had gone Mandy looked at Toby. Dad had set his broken leg with a special plastic bandage called a vetcast. It was much lighter than a plaster one and much better − especially for a puppy.

Toby pushed his little wet nose up against the bars of his cage and Mandy reached in and picked him up. Cuddling him made her feel a lot better. At last she could stand the suspense about Cally no longer.

'I'm going through,' she said to James.

She put Toby back in his cage and gave him a final pat just as the treatment room door opened and her dad stood there, white-coated and masked. There was a smear of blood on the apron he wore over his lab coat.

Mandy's eyes met his and her heart turned over. Then he reached up and drew down the mask that covered his face — and smiled. He looked past her and said to Jean, 'Ring the Hapwells and tell them everything's going to be all right.' Then he turned to Mandy. 'I suppose you'll want to see the patient,' he said.

Mandy nodded, unable to speak. She followed her father into the treatment room. Simon was laying the little patient gently on a bed of clean muslin. Cally was curled up and fast asleep. Both front paws and one hind leg were bandaged and there was a light wadding of bandage round her tummy. Mandy stood looking down at the frail little bundle of life. She brushed her tears away and turned to her dad.

'What happened?' she said.

Mr Hope scratched his head. 'Take one sharp piece of machinery and add one very adventurous kitten,' he said, 'That's all — just an accident.'

'But she'll be OK?'

'Cally?' said Mr Hope. 'Oh, she'll be fine. It looked a lot worse than it was. The only thing was, there wasn't much time. I think we'll keep her here overnight. She can go into the residential unit tomorrow if she's well enough.'

Mandy looked at her dad. It was at times like these that she knew that all she ever wanted to do was look after animals — maybe even be a vet like Mum and Dad.

Later that evening Mandy talked to Grandad about it as she helped him stack hay bales for the vegetable stalls. 'I don't see why you shouldn't be a vet,' Grandad said. 'If you work hard enough. It isn't an easy job, you know, quite apart from all that studying at college.'

'I know that,' said Mandy, 'but it's worth it, isn't it, Grandad?' She sneezed as a handful of hay came loose and tickled her nose.

Grandad chuckled. 'How would you like to have to look after a great big fellow like that?' he said. Mandy looked where he was pointing. A shire horse. It was pulling an enormous cartload of fenceposts and canvas across the field.

'Aye, Dan,' Grandad called to the man at the leading-rein. 'Duke's a grand sight.'

Dan Venables waved but kept on going. 'Won't stop, Tom,' he said. 'You know Duke can't bear to be near hay.'

Mandy looked at the huge shire horse with its great shaggy mane and plumy tail. Its hooves were enormous. Dan kept Duke's brasses and leathers shining and Duke had pride of place at every Welford Show.

Grandad shook his head. 'Funny, a great big horse like that but put him near hay and he starts to go right off — wheezing like my old dad's bellows. They used to call it the heaves when I was a lad around my dad's forge.' Grandad's father had been the village blacksmith.

Mandy forked up a drifting pile of hay and stuffed it back under the baling twine. Golden dust danced in the evening light. 'That's it,' said Grandad. 'That dust. Gets into a horse's lungs. Duke got shut in a hay barn once. Bad business. That's why Dan is so careful now. Some horses just don't like hay. Most of them aren't bothered.'

Mandy patted the ranks of the hay bales. 'The vegetables will look great on here,' she said. 'Especially your leeks, Grandad.'

Grandad chuckled. 'I reckon my leeks are the best in the county,' he said. 'Not wanting to boast, of course.'

Mandy laughed. 'Of course not.' It was nice to have Grandad home again.

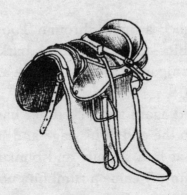

Four

By the time Mandy got home from school next day Cally the kitten was looking much better. Dad allowed Mandy to carry her carefully into the residential unit. The little bundle mewed piteously up at her and its tiny pink tongue rasped gently on her hand.

'There,' she murmured to the kitten as she laid her very gently on the bottom of an empty cage next to Toby's. 'You're going to be just fine now.'

Dad smiled. 'She'll be as fit as a flea in a few days. Just wait and see. The younger they are the better they recover.'

Mandy pushed a finger through Toby's cage and tickled his chin. The little dog barked happily. 'You've got company,' she said. 'Look after Cally for us, won't you.'

Toby barked again and licked her hand. Then he limped over to the end of his cage and snuffled. The kitten looked at him sleepily and blinked. From far down in her tummy came a rumbling noise. She was purring.

'See,' said Mr Hope, 'they've made friends.' He looked at his watch. 'Isn't it time you got down to some homework if you're going out for tea?'

Mandy groaned. But then she remembered what Grandad had said. If she wanted to be a vet she would have to work hard.

She met James at the Fox and Goose crossroads. She was in two minds about having tea with Susan. She hadn't been any friendlier today than she had yesterday. 'Quarter to six,' he said as she skidded her bike to a standstill. 'We'll make it easily.'

They got to The Beeches just before six. The nearer they got to the house the bigger it seemed to get. 'Whew!' said James. 'What a place.'

'Imagine wanting to live in London when you could live in that,' said Mandy. 'I think Susan's mum is daft.'

They turned their bikes into a courtyard at the front of the house. The house was built like a ranch with a veranda running round three sides of a courtyard. Its windows gleamed in the sun.

They got off their bikes and walked up the steps that gave on to the veranda. Mandy rang the front doorbell. A woman with a really frosty face answered. 'I'm Mrs Taylor,' she said. 'Susan is out riding. She should be back soon. Come in, but wipe your feet first.'

James looked scared to death and Mandy didn't blame him. The front door was wide open and she could see inside the house. The hall was floored with gleaming honey-coloured wood and the walls were sparkling white. At one end a big open tread staircase led to the upper floor.

The place was huge. Even the packing-cases piled neatly at one side of the hall looked impressive. But the house looked cold too. Mandy thought of Animal Ark and the cosy sitting-room with its red rugs and log fire. She shivered slightly. Maybe once Susan's family had moved in properly The Beeches would look a bit more welcoming.

She rubbed her hands on her jeans in case they were dirty and stepped forward. Just then there was the sound of hooves and Mandy swung round.

It was Susan — on her pony.

Mandy couldn't believe her own eyes. Then she ran down the steps of the veranda and threw her arms round the pony's neck. It hadn't been wishful thinking. It really had been Prince she had glimpsed in the paddock yesterday.

'It *is* you,' she said, nuzzling Prince's neck. 'It's really you. This is where you went. Oh, I've missed you so much.' She looked up at Susan, her eyes shining. 'I didn't know you had bought Prince,' she said. 'Oh, he's a wonderful pony.'

'You mean you know him?' said Susan. She didn't look too pleased.

Mandy nodded. 'Prince and I have known each other for years, haven't we, boy?' Prince whinnied and rubbed his head against Mandy's shoulder. 'I was wondering who Mrs Jackson had sold him to. I'm so glad he hasn't gone far away. Now I'll be able to come and visit him — that's if you'll let me. Oh, isn't he beautiful?' She stopped.

Susan was looking down at her, her face stiff. 'Yes, he is,' she said sharply. 'And he's mine.'

Mandy felt as if somebody had thrown a jug of cold water over her. What on earth had she said?

Susan dismounted and Mandy held the pony's head. She ran her hand over his flanks. They were steaming a little and damp to the touch. 'You'll have to rub him down,' she said. 'Jane always did after a ride. We used to—'

Susan looked at her. 'I don't care what you used to do,' she said. 'He's *my* pony now. Not Jane's. Just because you know him already doesn't give you the right to tell me how to look after him. I don't need you to tell me what to do.'

Mandy looked up. 'I didn't mean . . .' she stammered. 'Only he's hot.'

'Jim will see to him,' said Susan. 'Won't he, Mrs Taylor?'

Mrs Taylor sniffed. 'If I can find him,' she said.

Mandy remembered Susan telling her the gardener looked after her pony. That must be Jim. 'I can do it,' she said. 'I've rubbed Prince down lots of times. Jane showed me how. Please let me.'

Susan scowled. 'Jim will do it,' she said. 'And anyway tea will be ready, won't it, Mrs Taylor?'

'I'm just about to put it on the table,' said Mrs Taylor.

'Come on then,' said Susan.

Mandy gave Prince a last pat. 'See you later, boy,' she whispered. Prince whickered as Mandy followed Susan into the house. She hated leaving him so soon after finding him again.

Once inside, Mandy looked around. Through double doors at the side of the hall she caught a glimpse of heavy black and chrome dining-room furniture. It looked very smart but not welcoming. There was a pile of packing-cases in there too.

'We aren't having tea in there, are we?' James whispered in her ear.

'I hope not,' Mandy whispered back.

'Of course we haven't got everything sorted out yet,' Susan said, looking round the hall. 'Daddy is going to have interior decorators up from London.

'That'll be nice,' Mandy said weakly. Interior decorators. She and Mum and Dad had great fun painting and wallpapering the cottage when it needed it. Mandy was glad when Mrs Taylor took them down a passage behind the stairs and through a door at the back into the kitchen. She felt more at home there.

Tea was really good. Scrambled eggs and grilled tomatoes with lots of crusty bread and homemade scones to follow. Mrs Taylor could certainly cook.

'That was lovely,' Mandy said when they had finished.

'What do you want to do now?' Susan said.

'Let's go and see Prince,' Mandy said.

Susan frowned. 'You've seen him already.' She

turned to James, 'How would you like to see my new computer?'

James's face lit up. He really liked computers. Mandy sighed. Oh, well, she would see Prince again later.

They went up to Susan's bedroom. It was enormous. It had built-in furniture and a thick new-smelling carpet but the walls were bare. No posters or pictures.

But her computer was terrific — or so James said. Mandy wasn't very interested in computers. She wandered over to the window that looked out on to the courtyard and frowned. Prince was still there. It was very bad for him to be left sweating after a ride. She looked towards Susan. No use telling her. She would only tell Mandy to mind her own business.

As quietly as she could, Mandy slipped out of the room. It wasn't hard. James and Susan were too taken up with the computer to notice her.

She ran downstairs. At the bottom she hesitated, then made up her mind. She turned and made for the door to the kitchen. Mrs Taylor was busy at the oven. She looked up as Mandy came in.

'Mrs Taylor,' said Mandy. 'I'm just going to take Prince round to the stables and rub him down, if that's all right.'

Mrs Taylor looked at her and tutted. 'Is that pony still out there?' she said. 'I clean forgot about him. I meant to go and fetch Jim after I'd given you tea but this new-fangled cooker started playing up — as if I don't have enough to do. You go on, lass, and rub him down. He's got a cold as it is — or so young Susan says.'

'A cold?' Mandy said.

Mrs Taylor removed a cake from the oven and set it on a worktop. 'Susan says he coughs,' she said. 'But I don't know anything about horses and neither does Jim. It's a wonder Susan took the pony out today at all. She's been keeping him tucked up warm in the stable these last few days. I suppose he's company for her. I think she misses her mother. And I don't have time for her. It's as much as I can do to keep on top of the work in a big place like this. You go on and see to the pony.'

Mandy ran back through the hall and out into the courtyard. A cool breeze had got up. Gently she reached up and felt the pony's coat. Still damp — and cold now.

'Come on, boy,' she said, taking hold of his reins. 'Come on.' And she led him round the back of the house to the stables.

The stables were perfect. Everything you could

possibly need for looking after a pony was there. Currycombs and hay and water and pitchforks for turning over his bedding of straw. And the whole place smelled of fresh paint and newly cut wood. The stables were so new there were still piles of fine sawdust lying around.

'Not like your old stable, boy,' Mandy said. 'You've come up in the world.' But as she looked round the new stables she wondered if Prince missed the old lean-to in Mrs Jackson's orchard, the breeze rustling the trees and the smell of sweet grass.

Quickly she unsaddled the pony and hung up the tackle on its hooks. Then she set to — wiping him down, drying him off and finally giving his coat a really brisk brush.

'There,' she said when she had finished. 'That's better.'

She gave him a pat. He seemed warm again. She hoped he hadn't taken a chill. Once or twice he coughed. It worried Mandy. Prince had never been ill in his life. But it was warm in the stable and very dry. He wouldn't be chilled.

Mandy talked to the pony as she tidied up. Dust motes from the haynet danced in the sunlight coming in through the open stable door.

Just then a man came in. He was wearing boots

and carried a ball of twine and a rake. 'I thought I heard something,' he said. He looked at the pony. 'Nobody told me he was back.'

Mandy smiled. 'You must be Jim,' she said. 'It's all right. I've got him rubbed down. But he was out in the courtyard a long time. I hope he didn't get chilled.'

Jim shook his head. 'Nobody told me he was there,' he said. 'I usually put him straight in the stable when young Susan has finished riding him.'

Mandy smiled. 'And out in the paddock on fine days?' she said.

Jim shook his head. 'She won't have that,' he said. 'That pony's like gold to her. It's got to be in the stable warm and dry all the time.'

Mandy looked at Prince. 'He was coughing,' she said.

The gardener shook his head. 'Susan says he has a cold. I don't know much about horses,' he said. 'But there's been a good deal of new paint about this place and new paint always gives me a cold. So maybe horses are the same. It's the gardens I look after. I tell you, it's too much — gardens and a pony.'

Poor Prince, thought Mandy. Jim was too busy to have much time for him. And poor Susan. Mrs Taylor was too busy to have much time for *her*.

'I think he's all right now,' Mandy said. 'But I don't think you should water him for a while, not till he's really warmed up. It might chill him.'

'Little Miss Know-all,' said a voice from the door. It was Susan. 'Mrs Taylor told me you would be here. I told you, he's my pony. You've no right to be here without my permission.'

'I was only rubbing him down,' said Mandy. 'Mrs Taylor says he's got a cold.'

Susan frowned. 'It's only a little cold and he was fine when I had him out this afternoon. He didn't cough once.'

Mandy tried again. 'Prince has always been so healthy. It isn't like him. If you like, Dad can come and look at him. Or you could bring Prince over to Animal Ark.'

Susan's brows drew over. 'What a fuss. Don't tell me what to do with my own pony,' she said. 'He's mine, not yours. Just because you knew him before I did doesn't mean you own him. He's mine.'

Mandy felt her face go red. That was so unfair. Just then James appeared round the stable door. 'Maybe we should go,' he said when he saw Mandy's face.

Mandy dragged her eyes away from Susan. How could she be so possessive about an animal? Animals weren't toys or objects. They were real living creatures with personalities.

'OK,' she said to James. As she passed Susan she said carefully, 'Look, Susan, I was only trying to help. It's just that Prince isn't a bike or a pair of jeans or . . . or a computer, you know. You can't own animals the way you own things. It just isn't like that.'

Susan didn't say anything but she moved past Mandy and went to stand beside her pony.

Mandy gave up. 'Tell Mrs Taylor tea was lovely and thank you for asking us,' she said. 'Oh, I nearly forgot. Would you like to bring Prince over tomorrow to try the jumps for the pony trials at the Welford Show? They need somebody to pace them out — to make sure they've got the distances right.'

Susan moved towards the pony and put her arms round its neck. 'I might,' she said.

Mandy looked at her. Why was she so difficult? 'Oh, well,' she said. 'If you want to help we'll be there around seven.

Susan buried her head in the pony's neck. Her hair was almost the same colour as Prince's mane. Then she took a carrot out of her pocket and offered it to Prince.

No, thought Mandy as she looked at Prince's soft

brown mane, his gentle eyes. You didn't 'own' animals. Animals weren't things.

The pony whickered softly and daintly lifted the carrot from Susan's palm with velvety lips. There wasn't a computer in the world that could do that.

Five

Mandy and James went straight to the surgery at Animal Ark. Jean was just leaving. 'That little kitten's perked up amazingly,' she said. 'She's been trying to get her bandages off.'

Mandy laughed. 'That's a good sign,' she said.

'And young Tommy Pickard is in to see his hamsters,' said Jean. 'My but that little boy misses them something awful.'

'Any new animals tonight?' asked James.

Jean hunted around for her car keys and found them in her coat pocket. 'A budgie with an impacted crop, but your mum saw to that, Mandy. And Mrs

Ponsonby was in with Pandora.'

Mandy groaned. 'That poor little dog. She's so fat she can hardly move.'

Jean nodded. 'Your mum told her that. Mrs Ponsonby wasn't pleased.'

Mandy grinned. 'Good for Mum,' she said. 'I hope she gave her a telling-off.'

'Oh, I did,' said a voice from the surgery door. Mandy turned to see her mother standing there smiling, her red hair tied back from her face. 'Not that it'll do any good.'

'Mum,' said Mandy, 'do you think there are people who shouldn't have pets?'

Mrs Hope looked at her. 'Mrs Ponsonby is really fond of Pandora,' she said. 'If anything really bad happened to that little dog she would be devastated.' She sighed. 'Still, I wish I could persuade her to keep to a sensible diet.'

'Who?' said James, grinning. 'Mrs Ponsonby or Pandora?'

Mrs Hope laughed in spite of trying to look disapproving. Mrs Ponsonby was a very large lady.

'Oh, Mum,' said Mandy. 'You'll never guess — Susan's pony is Prince.'

'Prince!' said Mrs Hope. 'You've found him. Oh, Mandy, I'm so pleased.'

The telephone rang. Jean picked it up and spoke for a moment before handing it over to Mrs Hope. 'Calving,' she whispered.

Emily Hope spoke into the receiver. Mandy looked at her — suddenly all brisk efficiency and understanding. 'I'll be right there,' she said. 'Keep her warm and as quiet as possible. I'm on my way.'

'What is it?' said Mandy as her mother put the phone down.

'Baildon Farm,' said Mrs Hope. 'One of their Jersey heifers. She's just a little thing and it's her first calf.' She looked at the two upturned eager faces. 'Want to come?'

'Yes, please.' James and Mandy nodded eagerly.

'You haven't promised to help Grandad tonight, have you?'

James grinned. 'We've got the night off,' he said.

Mrs Hope smiled. 'Right,' she said. 'James, you phone home to let them know where you are, I'll get my bag and, Mandy, tell Dad where I'm going. Be at the car in two minutes flat.'

They scuttled to do as they were told. Mandy popped her head round the treatment room door. Dad was there with Walter Pickard and Tommy. The three hamsters were looking a bit bald but were lively enough to run up and down Tommy's sleeve.

'We'll keep them here a little longer,' Mr Hope was saying. 'Just to make sure they haven't swallowed any of that stuff. And remember, Tommy, just because you like chewing-gum doesn't make it good for hamsters.' The little boy nodded solemnly up at him, his eyes round, his mop of white blond hair dancing with every nod.

Mr Hope looked up. 'How was the pony?' he said to Mandy.

'You'll never believe this, Dad. It was Prince.' She laughed at her father's surprise. 'I was surprised too,' she said. 'Isn't it wonderful? The only thing is, he had a cough. But Susan thinks it's just a cold and the gardener says new paint gives him a cold too.'

'Probably is,' said Mr Hope. 'Paint does that sometimes. But if she's worried tell her I'll go over and see him.'

Mandy began to say 'I did' but Walter said, 'Is that the lass that's coming round to try our jumps?'

Mandy nodded. 'At least, she might,' she said. Just then she heard her mother's voice in Reception. 'James and I are going to a calving with Mum,' she said. 'Up at Baildon.'

Dad nodded. 'Molly, a Jersey heifer,' he said. 'One of your mum's favourites. She delivered that little heifer. Saved its life. She's always had a soft spot for it. Don't get in the way now.'

'We won't,' said Mandy. A car horn hooted. 'Got to go.'

Baildon Farm was high up on the moor. Mandy had been there a couple of times and it always seemed as if it was perched on the roof of the world. Mandy loved Baildon. From there you could look down on Welford and Walton sitting like toy villages far below.

Jack Mabson, the farmer, met them at the cowshed door. He looked worried. 'She's started, but she's so small . . .' he said to Mrs Hope. He was a big man but somehow he looked smaller than Mandy's mum just then.

Emily Hope gave him a reassuring pat on the arm. 'She's a fighter, Jack,' she said. 'She wouldn't be here now if she wasn't. We both know that.' She turned to Mandy and James. 'Besides, I've brought her some visitors. We can't disappoint them.'

Mandy was staring at the cowshed. From inside she heard a faint lowing sound. 'Mum . . .' she began but Mrs Hope was getting her bag, taking out the calving gown and getting into it. Its rubbery folds covered her from head to toe.

'Water, soap, towels?' she said to Jack Mabson.

'All ready,' he said. He was beginning to look less strained.

A rosy-cheeked woman came out of the house into the yard. 'Now then,' she said. 'How about some of my fruitcake?'

Mrs Hope looked at Mandy and James. 'You go ahead,' she said. 'I'll call you to see the calf.' She hurried into the cowshed with Jack.

Mandy and James went with Mrs Mabson into the big farm kitchen. There was a wood fire burning and two comfortable armchairs drawn up to it. On the scrubbed kitchen table was a huge fruitcake, still warm from the oven. It smelled wonderful. Mrs

Mabson poured a big mug of milk for each of them, but Mandy found her eyes going to the clock again and again. Minutes ticked by. Thirty, forty. She could hardly bear the suspense.

Just when she thought she would burst with the effort of sitting still there was a sound at the door and Jack Mabson came in. Mandy's heart stopped for a moment. Then she saw that his face was wreathed in smiles. 'A fine little heifer,' he said. 'Just like her mother.'

Mandy and James were up out of their chairs in a flash.

'Go on, then,' said Jack. 'It's a wonderful sight, that's for sure.'

They were out of the door and into the cowshed in an instant. 'Shh,' said Mandy as they went from the sunlight into the warm sweet-smelling shadows of the shed. Then she saw it − a newborn calf curled under its mother's front legs. Molly was licking her calf, coaxing her into wakefulness.

Mrs Hope stood by them proudly. Her calving gown was rolled up at her feet and she was pulling down her sleeves. 'Isn't she a beauty?' she said. 'Just like her mother.'

Mandy looked in wonder at the little calf. Its coat was golden where shafts of sunlight found their way into the cowshed. 'Oh, Mum,' she breathed.

'Do you want to stay for a while?' asked Mrs Hope. 'I think I'll try some of Mrs Mabson's cake and a cup of tea.'

Mandy nodded, her eyes shining.

'We'll be very quiet,' said James. 'We won't move a muscle.'

Mrs Hope laughed. 'I doubt if Molly would notice,' she said. 'She's too busy with this little one here.'

'What are you going to call her?' said Mandy just as Jack and his wife came into the cowshed.

Jack laughed. 'Now then,' he said. 'I reckon that's for you to say. Your mum's brought both them little heifers into the world. She gave Molly her name so I think it's only right you should have the naming of this little one.'

'Oh, thank you,' said Mandy. She turned to James. 'What shall we call her?'

James grinned. 'She's a girl. You choose,' he said.

'Goldie,' Mandy said as she watched the sun strike another patch of gold on the little calf's flank. 'We'll call her Goldie.'

What a day! She had found Prince and seen a newborn calf. What a wonderful day!

Six

Mandy was out of bed and down to the residential unit before breakfast next morning. She wanted to see how the kitten was getting on.

Mr Hope was in the treatment room. 'You're early this morning,' he said jokingly. 'How was the calf?'

Mandy spent a delicious ten minutes telling him about Goldie as she started cleaning out the small animals' cages. She stopped to help her father as he changed the dressing on Cally's hind leg. He picked up the little tortoiseshell kitten and tucked her firmly into the crook of his arm while Mandy smoothed some ointment on the bad gash in her leg.

'There,' she said gently to it, 'And don't go playing with sharp farm tools again.' The kitten mewed and tried to lick the ointment off its back leg but Mr Hope wound a fresh bandage deftly round the wound before it could get to it.

'She's bright this morning,' Mandy said. Then to the kitten she said. 'Look at Toby. He isn't making a fuss about his leg.' Toby the puppy looked up at her and wagged his tail. Mandy put the kitten gently back in her cage and picked him up. He licked her nose.

'And what about Prince? Do they want a visit?' Dad said.

Mandy put the puppy back and unlatched the hamsters' cage. She let one of them run up her sleeve. The little creature seemed to be doing well. 'No,' she said. 'Susan might be coming down to the show field tonight. I thought maybe . . .'

'I could just happen to drop by,' said Mr Hope.

Mandy turned to him. 'Oh, Dad, would you? I mean she might not even be there.'

'She looks after him all right, doesn't she?' said Mr Hope.

Mandy bit her lip. It felt like telling tales but then Prince was the important thing. 'The gardener is supposed to look after him but he doesn't know anything about horses. He told me so himself.'

Mr Hope came round and stood in front of her as she stroked Tommy's hamster. 'You know Prince has always been a healthy little pony,' he said. 'Strong as a horse, you might say.'

'Oh, Dad,' groaned Mandy. Her father was always saying stupid things.

'But seriously,' said Mr Hope, 'I don't think you have anything to worry about. I saw Prince only a few weeks ago when Mrs Jackson decided to sell him. He was absolutely fine then.'

'Not coughing?' said Mandy.

Mr Hope shook his head. 'Sound as a bell. But sometimes moving a pony from one home to another can upset it. Believe it or not, Mandy, Prince could just be taking a while to settle in. Odd little ailments aren't unusual in these circumstances. Ponies can be very sensitive creatures.'

'You mean he might be homesick?' said Mandy.

'He might be,' said Mr Hope. 'Sometimes animals pine – just like people.'

Mandy thought of Susan. Maybe she was taking a while to settle in too. Maybe she was homesick and that was what was making her so awkward. 'Prince certainly was very glad to see me,' said Mandy. *And*

Susan didn't like that, she thought.

'There then,' said Mr Hope. 'A familiar voice, a person he recognised. It sounds as if he might be pining a bit.'

Mandy smiled. 'That's probably all it is, Dad,' she said, 'But—'

'But I'll see him just as soon as I get the chance,' said Mr Hope. 'Only promise me one thing.'

'What?' said Mandy.

Dad ruffled her hair. 'Don't go getting yourself in a state about it. It's probably nothing at all.'

'OK,' said Mandy. 'I promise.' She gave the hamster a last cuddle and slid it back into its cage.

'Breakfast,' Mum called from the door. 'Just the two of us, Mandy. There's been a call for you, Adam. Metcalf's Farm. It's Shep. He's got one of his hind legs caught on some barbed wire and John Metcalf can't get him free without doing more damage.'

Mandy looked up. 'Poor Shep,' she said. Shep was the Metcalf's prize sheepdog. They had had him for years.

'He'll be OK,' Mrs Hope said. 'John is staying with him until Dad gets there, just to make sure he doesn't pull against the wire and hurt himself even more.'

Mr Hope was already on his way out of the door as Mandy and her mother sat down to breakfast. Mandy shook her head. A vet's life was certainly a busy one.

Breakfast was almost over when there was a tap at the door. Gran came bustling in with a letter in one hand and a bundle of rolled-up posters sticking out of her shoulder bag. Gran had really taken to writing letters since she'd started the village campaign to save their post office. She waved the letter at them. 'She's coming,' she said. 'She said yes.'

Mum smiled and reached another cup and saucer down from the dresser behind her. 'Who's coming where?' she said to Gran.

Mandy grinned. She watched as Gran sat herself down and pulled a bundle of handbills and posters out of her bag. She spread them on the table. Mum made space for the cup and saucer and poured a cup of tea.

'Miranda Jones,' Gran said, taking a sip of tea. 'Mmm, that's lovely. Just what I needed.' She unrolled one of the posters. Across the top in big letters were the words 'WELFORD SHOW' and underneath was a list of all the events. Gran stabbed a finger at some words at the bottom of the page: 'PRIZES TO BE PRESENTED BY'.

'The Committee left some posters blank till the very last minute,' said Gran, 'hoping she would say yes. We just put "a local celebrity" on the first batch. So, all we have to do now is fill in 'MIRANDA JONES' along the bottom here and we can start putting up the posters and handing out leaflets.'

Mandy took a leaflet from the pile. There was a gap at the bottom of those too. 'Do you have to fill in the name on all of these?' she said. 'It'll take you ages.'

Gran's eyes twinkled. 'I thought you might give me a hand,' she said. 'You could give them out at school and put up some posters between here and Welford.'

Mandy laughed. 'OK,' she said.

Mrs Hope was studying the poster. 'And what does Mrs Ponsonby say about this?' she said.

Gran took another sip of tea and said casually, 'Oh, she doesn't know yet. I mean there was no point in telling her until we were sure. Besides, nobody had actually asked her to give out the prizes.'

'Nobody ever does,' said Mrs Hope, 'but she does it every year. She must think she's the local celebrity.'

'Mmm,' said Gran and had another sip of her tea.

'You do make really good tea, Emily. Now tell me, how is your talk going?'

Mandy giggled. Gran was really good at changing the subject when it suited her. Even Mum gave in.

'It's going really well,' said Mrs Hope. 'I've nearly finished writing it. Now all I have to do is learn it.'

'What's it about, Mum?' said Mandy. Mrs Hope had been asked to give a talk to a conference for vets in York quite soon. Mandy was really proud of her. Imagine all those vets listening to her mum!

'Allergies,' Mrs Hope said. 'Animals get allergies just like people do and with all these new pesticides and fertilisers around farmers have to be very careful.'

'What kind of allergies?' Mandy said.

Mum shrugged. 'All kinds,' she said. 'Skin rashes, stomach upsets, breathing problems.'

'What, like asthma?' said Mandy. Kate had asthma and when she got an attack she was really breathless. She had been taken to hospital a few times when it was really bad. Mandy knew it could be dangerous.

'Like that,' said Mrs Hope, 'but there's one I'm quite interested in. It's called SAD.'

'SAD?' said Mandy.

Mum nodded. 'It stands for Small Airway Disease. It's like Chronic Obstructive Pulmonary Disease but SAD is easier to say. People used to have different names for it — broken wind or the heaves.'

'Grandad was talking about the heaves the other day,' said Mandy. 'Duke has that.'

Mrs Hope nodded. 'Duke didn't always have it. It can come on at any time really.'

There was a familiar sound outside — gravel spurting and a bicycle bell pinging. James. Mandy stood up.

'Don't forget these,' said Gran, thrusting a pile of handbills and posters at her.

Mandy stuffed them in her schoolbag. 'When is this talk, Mum?' she said as she tried to get all the leaflets and posters into her bag.

Mrs Hope sighed. 'Saturday, unfortunately,' she said.

Mandy stopped, all thoughts of posters and allergies banished from her mind. 'But you'll miss the Welford Show,' she said.

Mrs Hope nodded. 'It can't be helped,' she said.

Mandy looked at her sympathetically. 'That's really bad luck, Mum,' she said.

'Your dad will be there,' Mrs Hope said. 'He'll be on duty. It's his turn this year.'

'What a pity,' said Gran. 'You'll miss Miranda Jones giving out the prizes. She's my favourite. I just love *Parson's Close*.'

'Mmm,' said Mrs Hope, '*if* Miranda Jones is doing it.'

'What do you mean, "if"?' said Gran but she didn't sound as confident as usual.

Mandy grinned as she shot out of the door to meet James. Thank goodness she wouldn't be around when Mrs Ponsonby found out she wasn't the local celebrity after all!

Seven

Mandy got a lovely surprise on the way to school. Prince was in the paddock of The Beeches, kicking up his heels and cantering round the field. 'Look,' she said to James and they drew their bikes into the side of the road.

Mandy leaned over the fence and called the pony's name. At once his ears pricked up and he came trotting across the short turf towards her. She put her arms round his neck. 'Hello, boy,' she said and he whickered and snuffled at her hair. Mandy giggled. 'That tickles,' she said to him.

'Someone's coming,' James said.

Mandy looked up. Jim, the gardener, was walking down the paddock towards them. He gave them a wave. 'Got to take him back now,' he said. 'I only let him out while I mucked out his stable. I don't get time to do it very often.'

Mandy rubbed Prince's nose. 'What a shame,' she said. 'Do you have to? He seems so happy out here.'

'Susan's orders,' said Jim. 'She doesn't want his cold to get worse.'

'Oh, well,' said Mandy. 'I suppose he has to keep warm but really he seems fine.' And he did. There was no sign of a cough. 'I'm glad about that anyway,' Mandy said to James as they watched Jim lead Prince away. 'He really does seem much better.'

She said so to Susan when she saw her at school. Susan frowned. 'He shouldn't be out at all,' she said. 'I want him in good condition for the Welford Show.'

'You're entering then?' said Mandy.

Susan sniffed. 'I'd better,' she said. 'After all, my mother is going to be doing the prize giving. She phoned me this morning to tell us. I've decided to enter Prince in the jumps.'

'Oh, good,' said Mandy. 'My gran is really pleased.'

Susan gave her a puzzled look and opened her

mouth to say something but Miss Potter called the class to order and started the geography lesson so it wasn't until break that Susan grabbed Mandy's arm and said. 'What's your gran got to do with me entering Prince in the trials?'

'Not the trials. The prize giving,' Mandy said. 'The Women's Institute wrote to your mum asking if she would come and do it since she's got connections with Welford now. We can put her name on the posters.'

Susan looked as if she didn't know whether to be annoyed or not.

'She's famous, isn't she?' said Mandy.

'Of course she's famous,' Susan said.

'Well, then,' said Mandy, 'It'll be good for the show.'

Susan looked undecided. 'And I'm glad you're entering Prince,' Mandy went on. 'They give marks for grooming, you know. I could help you with that if you like.'

For a moment she thought Susan was going to say 'Don't bother' or 'It's none of your business'. Then she saw a change come over her face. Susan's eyes lit up. 'If I won then Mum would be giving the prize to me, wouldn't she?'

Mandy nodded. 'I suppose so.'

Susan's eyes grew dreamy. 'I *will* enter, then' she said. 'And I'll win.' And with that she marched off to her next class.

Mandy didn't see much of her for the rest of the day but she was so busy writing in 'MIRANDA JONES' in big letters and doling out handfuls of leaflets and posters to people that she hardly noticed.

'Why is it Miranda *Jones*?' Melanie said. 'Susan's name is Collins.'

'Jones is her stage name,' said Mandy.

Melanie sniffed. 'Not very fancy, is it? It should be something romantic or posh — like Honeychurch or Smythe-Bassington-Jones.'

Mandy shook her head. She was glad it wasn't Miranda Smythe-Bassington-Jones. It would take too long to write.

She caught up with James at lunch-time. 'I've done all mine,' he said. 'Now it's just the ones we've to stick up on the way home from school.'

'Great,' said Mandy. 'See you at half past three. I've still got a few more to give out.'

By the time half past three came all the kids from the outlying districts had their posters to put up in the villages and farms. It took Mandy and James three times longer than usual to get from Walton to Welford. They had put up posters at the end of every farm road.

Prince wasn't in the paddock when they passed The Beeches. But she hoped she would see him tonight. It was a pity he had to be inside on such a lovely day. Maybe he missed that. Jane had always put him out to crop grass in fine weather.

'There,' said Mandy as they posted the last one at the Fox and Goose. 'Nobody could miss them. It should be a great turnout for the show.'

Mr Hardy, the owner of the Fox and Goose, came out to admire it. 'Aye' he said, 'that looks grand. And if you give me some handbills I'll see they're left where people can get them.'

'Thanks, Mr Hardy,' Mandy said, handing him a wodge of handbills.

Mr Hardy looked at their red faces. 'Thirsty work, that,' he said. 'You sit yourselves down and I'll fetch you a glass of lemonade.'

They got off their bikes and settled themselves on the bench outside the pub. In a moment two hands appeared out of the open window above James's shoulder. The hands were clasping two brimming glasses of lemonade and two bags of crisps.

Mandy smiled. 'Thanks, Mr Hardy.'

'We could do with these,' said James, taking the glasses.

Mr Hardy leaned over the window ledge and winked. 'As I said, thirsty work,' he said to them. 'Cheers!'

They were still sitting on the bench polishing off the last of the lemonade when Mrs Ponsonby came by on her way to the village hall.

Mrs Ponsonby was a large woman with a blue rinse and pink spectacles. She came down the street like a ship in full sail. She was carrying a large bundle of bunting under one arm and a very fat Pekinese under the other. She looked at them as she passed and tutted disapprovingly. 'Whatever would your grandmother say, Mandy Hope,' she said. 'Sitting outside a public house in broad daylight.'

'It would be worse sitting outside a public house in the dark,' James muttered. But Mrs Ponsonby didn't hear for at that moment the peke gave a shrill yap and tried to make a dive for Mandy's crisps.

'Now, now, Pandora my precious,' Mrs Ponsonby said. Then she noticed the poster stuck up on the door of the Fox and Goose. 'What's this?' she said. It was one of James's posters. He had written Susan's mum's name in great big red letters with a felt-tipped pen. Mrs Ponsonby opened her mouth twice but she

WELFORD
SHOW
1.00 pm SAT 1st
Raffle Tombola
Pet Corner
HORSE SHOW CAKES
Refreshments
PRIZES TO BE
PRESENTED BY
MIRANDA
JONES
...ssion 50p

was so mad she couldn't speak. Then she got her
voice back. 'Miranda Jones,' she said. 'MIRANDA
JONES. The others said a local celebrity. Who is
Miranda Jones?'

'She's on TV,' Mandy said. 'In *Parson's Close*.
She's the vicar's wife. She's famous. Her husband
has bought that big new house on the Walton road.
That's what makes her "local".'

Mandy stopped as Mrs Ponsonby looked at her.
Pandora yelped. Mrs Ponsonby must have tightened
her grip.

'And whose idea was this?' she said. 'No, don't tell
me. I can guess.' She loosened her grip on Pandora
and shook the bundle of bunting at them. 'We'll see
about this,' she said. 'We'll just see about this.' And
she turned on her heel and marched off majestically
down the hill to the village hall.

'I pity your poor gran,' said James.

Mandy smiled. 'Somehow I don't think Gran will
be too bothered. The WI committee decided to ask
Susan's mum. They're all fed up with Mrs
Ponsonby.' She sighed. 'It's Pandora I feel sorry
for.'

'Why does she carry her everywhere?' said James.
'Why doesn't she let her walk?'

Mandy sighed. 'Poor Pandora is too fat to walk

very far,' Mandy said. 'Mrs Ponsonby overfeeds her. She even gives her chocolates. It's so bad for her teeth.'

'Oh, well,' said James. 'If I don't go I won't be fed at all.' He got up. 'See you tonight,' he said. 'Seven o'clock at the field.'

'Mmm,' said Mandy, getting up reluctantly. Sitting in the sun drinking lemonade really was nice. Then she remembered Cally and Toby and Tommy's hamsters and wondered if there were any new animals at Animal Ark today. She was up and on to her bike like a shot. 'See you later,' she called as she whizzed down the track towards home.

There was a new patient at Animal Ark. A guinea-pig.

'Go in and see it,' said Simon. 'Your dad won't mind. He's got Johnny Foster and three of his friends in there already. Johnny Foster was nine and lived near James.

Mandy slipped into the treatment room and caught her dad's eye. 'What's wrong with him?' she said as she approached the treatment table. Four boys stood around the table looking at the guinea-pig.

'He's losing weight,' said Mr Hope and turned to Johnny. 'What do you feed him on?'

Johnny drew himself up. 'All the best things,' he

said. 'Food from the pet shop in Walton and carrots and lettuce and apple. But he doesn't want to eat anything. He's so thin. I'm scared he's going to die.'

Mr Hope laid a hand on Johnny's shoulder. 'Now look, Johnny,' he said. 'Your guinea-pig isn't going to die. I promise you that but do you see these teeth?' Mr Hope pointed at the two sharp incisor teeth. Johnny nodded. 'Guinea-pigs' teeth aren't like ours,' Mr Hope said. 'They grow all the time. When they get too long it makes it difficult for them to eat. They need something to wear their teeth down. A block of wood will do, just so long as he can rasp his teeth against it and get a good chew.'

'Will he have to go to the dentist and get them out?' said Johnny.

Mr Hope laughed. 'No,' he said. 'All I have to do is clip them. He won't feel it. His teeth aren't like ours. It's just like cutting your fingernails.'

Johnny didn't look convinced.

'Look,' said Mr Hope, 'You watch me and if you think I'm hurting him then I'll stop right away.'

He gave the guinea-pig to Mandy. 'Hold him,' he said. He selected a pair of small stainless steel clippers form the sterilising unit. A couple of quick snips and it was done. Mandy gave the guinea-pig a tickle

under the chin. He really was very thin. Then she
handed him to Johnny.

At once Johnny dived into his pocket and brought
out a rather dusty-looking piece of carrot. The
guinea-pig eyed it for a moment and then seized on
it. It was gone in seconds. Johnny's face lit up.

'He's hungry again,' he said. 'He's eating!'

And he and his three friends trooped out of the
treatment room.

'Feeding animals properly is really important, isn't
it, Dad?' Mandy said. She was thinking of Mrs
Ponsonby's dog.

'Feeding people is pretty important too,' said Mr
Hope. 'That was my last patient. Let's get washed
up. Your mum's been out all day doing tuberculin
injections and she'll be exhausted so we're going to
give her a treat. You and I are going to make dinner.'

Mandy and her dad got busy in the kitchen and by
the time Mum came in dinner was nearly ready.

Mrs Hope was delighted. 'This is wonderful,' she
said as she sat down at the table.

They chattered over dinner. Mum had managed to
call in at Baildon. 'Goldie sends her love,' she said.
'And there's something in my coat pocket for you,
Mandy.'

Mandy raced out to the hall and burrowed in her

mother's pockets. She felt a thin piece of card which she drew out and there she was. Goldie, the calf, standing sturdy and strong beside her mother.

'Look, Dad,' she said as he came out to the hall after her. 'It's Goldie, the new calf. Mr Mabson must have taken a Polaroid of it.'

Dad looked at the picture and smiled. 'That's one that's going to get pride of place on your wall,' he said. Then he lowered his voice. 'Look, Mandy,' he said. 'Your mum's really tired so I think she should get straight to bed and have a good night's rest. So that means I have to be here on call.'

Mandy nodded. 'So you won't be able to come down to the field to see Prince?' she said. She smiled. 'It's all right, Dad. I saw him this morning on my way to school and he was his old self again.'

Mr Hope smiled. 'In any case I'll see him at the show,' he said. 'I'm on duty, remember?'

Mandy agreed. But there would be no need. Prince was better now.

Eight

James was already there when Mandy got down to Redpath's field just before seven o'clock. He was sitting on the churchyard wall waiting for her. 'It's looking good,' he said.

Mandy looked around. It certainly was looking good. There were several tents and marquees up already, bunting was fluttering from trestle tables set up around the edges of the field and everywhere there were groups of people hammering stalls together, roping off areas of the field, setting up tombola stands and piling bales of hay into tiers for the coconut-shy. Over on the far side Mandy could see her grandad and Walter Pickard. She waved to them and Grandad beckoned her over.

'Ready for some hard work?' he said as they reached them.

Mandy and James nodded and Grandad handed them a bucket of water and a brush each. 'Right,' he said. 'First thing to do is get these jumps washed down. They've got to be in tip-top condition for Saturday.'

'Even the one made out of hay bales?' James joked.

Grandad grinned. 'No, I reckon you can leave that one,' he said.

Mandy and James started work. The jumps were spaced round the area that had been roped off for the pony trials. They scrubbed at them with the long-handled brushes. The red and white poles stretched across their supports became brighter. Even the painted bricks of the 'wall' jumps shone brick red. It was hard work but they were enjoying being part of the team working to make the show a success.

They had almost finished when Mandy heard a car pull up. She turned to see a dark green horse box towed by a blue Jaguar draw into the field. Susan. That was her dad's car.

Mandy put down her brush. 'James,' she said,

'Susan's arrived with Prince.'

James looked up from a five-bar gate he was scrubbing. 'Just so long as she doesn't get these jumps dirty,' he said. 'I'm exhausted.'

Mr Collins was unlocking the horse box and letting down the ramp. Mandy stood, brush in hand, and watched as Prince stepped delicately down the ramp and on to the grass. She saw his head go up sniffing the air and then he coughed. 'He's coughing again,' she said to James. 'He was fine this morning. I wish Dad had been able to come down after all.'

James looked at her. 'You know what your dad said. Prince has always been a healthy pony.'

Mandy pursed her lips. 'He doesn't sound too healthy now.'

Susan took Prince's halter and led him to the edge of the ring, tethering him to a post. Then she walked off towards where Grandad and Walter were talking to some other helpers.

'Come on,' said Mandy. 'Let's go and see him.'

Dropping her brush, she sprinted across to where Prince was tethered. As she approached he coughed again but not as deeply as he had before. She felt his flank. It was warm and dry. As she ran her hand gently down the pony's side some hay dust rose from his coat in a little cloud.

'He needs a good brushing,' said James but Mandy wasn't listening. She had her ear pressed close to Prince's flank. She could hear the breath deep in his chest. Was it her imagination or did it sound odd, not steady the way it usually was? She turned a troubled face to James.

'Is there something wrong with him?' said James.

Mandy just shook her head in puzzlement and continued stroking Prince's flank. As she did so she felt his breath steady. She rubbed his nose and his ears twitched towards her. 'How are you, boy?' she said.

Prince nuzzled her shoulder and whickered. 'That's odd,' said Mandy. 'He seems all right now. Yet I'm sure his breathing was funny before.'

'Here comes Susan,' said James.

Susan was striding across the field towards them. She was carrying a saddle. 'I'm going to try the jumps now,' she said.

'I'll help you saddle up,' said Mandy.

For a moment she thought Susan was going to refuse her help. But Susan just said, 'If you like,' and slung the saddle over Prince's back.

As they adjusted the girth and let down the stirrups Mandy said carefully, 'He was coughing again.'

'I know,' said Susan. She looked puzzled. Mandy

tried to hide her surprise. Maybe she wasn't going to fly at her for interfering. 'But Jim let him out for a while today — you saw him. Maybe he got chilled.' She looked at the pony. 'But he's all right now, isn't he?'

Mandy had to agree. There seemed to be nothing wrong with the pony. 'See how he goes over the jumps,' she said. 'If you don't think he's fit you don't have to do it. You don't have to enter him in the trials at all.'

Susan looked at her in disbelief. 'Not enter him?' she said. 'Who said anything about not entering him? Of course I'm going to enter him. I've got to. I tell you I'm going to make Mum so proud of me she'll—' She stopped.

'What?' said Mandy but just then Grandad and Walter arrived. What was it Susan had been going to say?

'Why don't you walk him round the jumps first,' Grandad was saying to Susan. 'Just to see if we've got the spacing about right. Then we can put him to the fences.'

Mandy watched as Susan led Prince away. First she showed him each jump, letting him take his time investigating it, getting to know it. Then she got up on him and walked him round the course, just skirting the fences, pacing them, getting the feel of the layout. And only then did she urge him into a trot and then a canter round the outskirts of the field before bringing him up to the jumps at the gallop.

The first two jumps went smoothly. Prince sailed over them, his tail arching gracefully, his hooves clearing the bars by centimetres. At the third he was wrongfooted and Susan turned him easily aside and slowed him to a trot before trying it again. Once again he was wrongfooted, half a pace out on the approach. Susan slowed him to a walk this time.

'I think this one is a bit out,' she called to Grandad. 'The angle coming into the fence doesn't seem right.'

Grandad and Walter went into a huddle then moved the jump back a bit and to the side so that the angle was wider. 'Try that,' Grandad called back to her.

Susan took a long slow approach to the fence, giving Prince plenty of time to refuse, not forcing him. He flew over it like a dream.

The only other fence that gave Prince any trouble was the fifth jump. The one made of hay bales. He simply refused it. Susan was clearly puzzled. She tried him three times in all. The third time Prince took the jump but he wasn't happy. His head came up, straining at the bit as he came over.

After that Prince had no trouble. Susan leaned over and patted him as they cleared the last jump. Mandy saw her bend to whisper in his ear. Prince seemed absolutely fine, hardly out of breath but then Susan had taken the jumps easily, giving him time where he needed it, not pushing him on from jump to jump.

'She's good, isn't she?' said James.

Mandy nodded. She was surprised. Susan boasted so much about everything it was hard to believe she really was good at showjumping. 'She's better than Barry Prescott,' Mandy said. Barry sometimes forced Star.

'Look,' said Mandy. Susan had taken Prince right round the outside of the jumps. She was going to go for a full circuit. Mandy saw her turn Prince at the far end of the field, gather the reins firmly in her hands and point him towards the first jump.

Mandy held her breath. Susan and the little pony seemed to melt into each other. Looking at her as she cleared first one fence, then the next, Mandy couldn't imagine Susan ever falling off — or Prince ever failing to clear a jump.

Then as they thundered up the field towards Mandy and James, Mandy saw Prince's head go up. He was trying to turn away from the hay bales. Horse and rider faced them head on. Mandy saw Susan's mouth set, saw her gather the reins more tightly, touch her heels to the pony's flanks — and he was over. But his eyes were rolling.

Susan and Prince were round the top of the field, heading for the last three jumps. Prince cleared them but Mandy was running towards the finish with James behind her.

'What's wrong?' he yelled as he pelted after her.

'Didn't you see his eyes?' Mandy shouted back. 'He didn't want to try that jump. He isn't happy.'

Susan was drawing Prince to a walk as they arrived. She slowed him to a halt. 'Pretty good,' she said, 'but he should be able to do even better.'

Mandy laid a hand on Prince's flank. She felt his chest plunge and ripple.

'It was too much for him,' she panted. 'Look at him. He's so out of breath.'

Susan looked down at her. Her smile had disappeared. 'Oh, come on,' she said. 'He's just jumped a clear round. You would be out of breath if you had done that. You're out of breath as it is and you've only run half the length of the course.'

Mandy bit her lip. It sounded so reasonable but she had watched Jane jump Prince many times. She had never seen Prince as out of breath as this.

'She's got a point,' said James.

Mandy turned to him. 'Whose side are you on?' she said.

James looked surprised. 'Nobody's,' he said. 'It isn't about taking sides, is it?'

Susan smirked down at Mandy. 'It *is* as far as Mandy's concerned.' She patted Prince's neck. 'Come on, Prince,' she said, 'At least *I* think you did well even though some people think you aren't up to it.'

'It isn't that,' said Mandy. Then she stopped. After all it was what she was saying — that Prince wasn't up to it.

Grandad and Walter came up to them.

'That was fine,' said Walter, 'and thanks for your help, Susan.'

Susan smiled down at him. 'He's a good jumper, isn't he?' she said.

Walter smiled. 'He is that,' he said.

'He's a grand little jumper,' said Grandad but Mandy saw him looking at the pony. Prince was still breathing heavily and Grandad was looking at his flanks, puzzled.

'Aye,' said Walter. 'The only better jumper in these parts is that bay gelding of young Barry Prescott's. He usually walks off with the prize in the jumping. He's fast, you see.'

Susan slid down off Prince and looked at them. 'Not this year he won't,' she said. 'You'll see. Prince can jump faster than that. Just you wait till the show. Now that I know he can clear the jumps, all he needs is a bit more speed.'

'Susan,' said Mandy.

Susan had begun to walk Prince towards the horse box. She turned to Mandy. 'What is it now?' she said.

Mandy took a deep breath. 'You won't push Prince too hard at the show, will you?' she said.

'Because you don't think he's up to it?' said Susan

scornfully. 'You just can't bear to see me win. But we will win, Mandy Hope. You'll see. All he had was a little cold and of course he's out of breath jumping. A day in a warm dry stable and he'll be fit for anything. He can go faster than that. I know he can. Barry Prescott won't win this year. I will — whatever happens.' And, her face grim with determination, she unsaddled Prince and led him into the horse box.

Mandy looked as Susan tethered the pony. There was a haynet secured at the far end of the box and Mandy plucked a handful and began rubbing Prince down. Then she dropped the hay to the floor of the box. Prince stamped and coughed. Susan turned to Mandy.

'It's just a cold,' she said and, walking down the ramp, began to secure the back door of the box.

As Mandy turned away she saw Susan's father come out of the marquee at the far end of the field and begin to walk towards the car. She wandered over to where she had left Grandad. He was still standing there. He looked thoughtful.

'What's the matter, Grandad?' she said.

Grandad scratched his head. 'I'm not sure,' he said. 'It was when I was standing there looking at Prince. It reminded me of something but I can't for the life of me remember what it is.' He shook his head. 'Old age, Mandy,' he said. 'I must be getting past it.'

Mandy smiled but she wasn't really paying attention. All she could think of was Susan's last words. She would win, whatever happened. Mandy would speak to her father again. He was on duty at the show. He *had* to look at Prince before the jumping. She hated to think what would happen if Susan rode Prince flat out. She remembered the panic and fear in Prince's eyes. A cold chill seemed to settle on her heart.

Nine

It was Saturday morning — the day of the Welford Show. Mandy was looking forward to seeing Prince. He hadn't been out in the paddock at all yesterday when they passed to and from school and Mandy hadn't dared to ask Susan how he was in case she snapped her head off. In any case, Susan was keeping out of her way.

Mandy jumped out of bed and dived for the bathroom. A quick shower, a clean pair of jeans and a fresh shirt and she was off, taking the stairs two at a time.

Mum was checking her papers for the conference and Dad was checking on the animals in the

residential unit. 'Are you taking Toby to the show?'
he asked Mandy as he came out of the surgery.

'What about his leg, Dad?' she said.

Dad smiled. 'Come and see,' he said.

Mandy followed him into the unit. There was
Toby in his cage − with no cast on his leg. 'He's
better,' she said.

Dad nodded. 'Good as new,' he said. 'The leg will
need a good deal of exercise but he's young so it
won't be long before he's running around as good as
new.'

'Then he doesn't need to stay in here any longer,'
Mandy said.

Mr Hope laughed. 'Bring him through,' he said.

Mandy set Toby down on the floor. He was still a
bit unbalanced but that was only because he wasn't
used to having four fully working legs yet. It
wouldn't be long before he was racing around.

Mr Hope said he would check Prince out just as
soon as he arrived at the show. Mandy felt as if a
weight had been lifted off her. She knew her father
wouldn't let Prince overstrain himself.

'What are his symptoms?' Mum asked.

'He gets really out of breath when Susan jumps
him,' said Mandy.

'Jumping is hard work,' said Mrs Hope.

Mandy shook her head. 'I know,' she said slowly, 'but he coughs sometimes when he's just standing still. It doesn't seem to make any sense.'

Mrs Hope gathered up the rest of her papers and looked at her watch. 'I'd better go,' she said, 'or I'll be late.' Then she hesitated, looking at the papers in her hand. 'You know,' she said, 'it could be an allergy of some sort.'

'Would that be serious?' said Mandy.

Mum frowned. 'It might be. It depends what kind of allergy you're talking about. It's a complicated business.'

Mr Hope smiled. 'Your head is full of allergies this morning,' he said. 'But I'll check it out.'

'I suppose you're right,' said Mrs Hope.

Mandy and her father went to the door to wave goodbye to Mum.

'Tommy Pickard is coming to collect his hamsters this morning,' Mr Hope said.

Mandy grinned. 'He wants to put them in the Family Pets section at the show.' She thought for a moment. 'Who's judging it?'

Mr Hope coughed. 'I am,' he said.

Mandy shook her head. 'You were keeping that a secret,' she said. 'Poor Dad. What a job!'

'And I'll know most of the animals as well as the

owners,' Mr Hope said. 'I wish they had asked somebody else.' He sighed. 'Maybe I'll just close my eyes, turn round three times and point. Anyway, let's get a move on.'

They didn't have any time to spare. By half past nine when James arrived they had done all the medications and finished the dressings.

James had Blackie with him. Dad gave the black Labrador a pat and Blackie looked up at him adoringly. Blackie was a typical Labrador, friends with the whole world.

'How are the tricks coming on, James?' asked Mr Hope.

James grinned. 'Watch,' he said. He took a big red hankie from his pocket, held it under Blackie's nose and disappeared into the hall with it. Then he came back and said to Blackie, 'Find!'

Blackie looked up at him, waved his tail, barked and licked his hand.

'Find!' said James again.

Blackie woofed delightedly and his tail wagged even faster.

Mr Hope laughed. 'You've got a long way to go there, James,' he said.

James shook his head. 'He just doesn't seem to get the message.'

'Unless it's feathers,' Mandy said and she and James laughed.

'I've got to dash,' Mr Hope said. He turned to Mandy. 'Can you hang on until Tommy gets here to collect the hamsters?'

Mandy nodded. 'No problem. You go on ahead.'

'Right,' said Mr Hope, picking up his bag and making for the door.

Mandy was smiling. 'Dad, wouldn't it be better to change out of your slippers?'

Mr Hope looked down. 'Thanks, Mandy. I'd look a real idiot turning up in these, wouldn't I?' He found his shoes, shoved his feet into them and picked up the slippers.

Mandy took them from him. 'Go,' she said, almost shoving him out of the door. 'You'll be late.'

'I'm going,' he said. He grabbed his bag and went out through the surgery door.

Mandy put the slippers neatly in a corner and she and James followed to wave goodbye.

Mandy ran after the car. 'Don't forget to have a look at Prince,' she shouted.

Mr Hope waved. 'I'll remember,' he said. 'Don't worry.'

'See you later,' called Mandy. She looked around her. 'Where's Toby?'

'Where's Blackie?' said James.

They soon tracked them down — in the sitting-room. In his hurry, Mr Hope had left the door between the surgery and the house open. Mandy looked at what had once been one of her dad's best slippers. It was a mangled mess. Toby looked guilty and dropped the slipper.

Mandy picked up the puppy and looked into its big brown eyes. 'Oh, you naughty thing,' she said, cuddling it. The puppy licked her nose and wagged his stumpy tail.

James picked up the slipper. 'Tell me your dad didn't really like these slippers,' he said.

Mandy made a face. 'They were his favourites,' she said. 'I don't know what he'll say.'

'Can I have my hamsters now?' said a little voice from the doorway. It was Tommy Pickard. 'The door was open so I just came in,' he said.

'Wait here,' said Mandy. 'I'll fetch them.

She went through to the surgery and collected the hamster cage. As she came back she carefully shut the door between the surgery and the house. 'There,' she said, giving the cage to Tommy,

Just then James gave a yell. 'He's done it! He's found the hankie! Good boy, Blackie. Good boy.' He put his arms round Blackie's neck.

'Oops.' Tommy said. 'I didn't mean to.'

Mandy looked round. The cage door was wide open. The three hamsters shot out.

'Tommy!' said Mandy, then she stopped as she saw what was happening.

One hamster was halfway up the curtains, another had gone under the sofa and the third was burrowing under the fireside rug. Toby looked as if he couldn't decide which one to chase first. Blackie just sat there for a moment, then he dropped the red hankie and started to pull at the fireside rug.

'Get Toby!' Mandy yelled to James.

James made a dive for the puppy, missed and fell flat on his face — across the hearthrug. A very startled hamster shot out from underneath and halfway up the leg of Mandy's jeans. She grabbed the hamster and thrust it into Tommy's hands.

'Put it back in the cage,' she said to him, 'and shut the door.'

The little boy's eyes were wide. 'OK,' he said.

'Got you,' said James as he finally grabbed hold of Toby. His face was red, his hair was standing on end and his glasses were knocked sideways — but he had the puppy.

Mandy managed to coax the second hamster out

from under the sofa. She went and put that one in the cage.

Tommy was sitting there watching the cage — as if the hamsters might break out again. 'Don't move,' Mandy said to him. She took Toby from James and gave him to Tommy. 'Hold him,' she said.

James was standing on a chair trying to reach the last hamster — the one that had shot up the curtains. But the hamster just sat there staring at him until he got too near — then it scampered along to the other end of the curtain rail.

Blackie was following the hamster's movements

with his eyes. Mandy couldn't help it. She started to laugh.

'What's so funny?' said James.

Mandy wiped away tears of laughter. 'You,' she said. 'Every time you get anywhere near it it just runs away. And then you have to move the chair. And then it runs to the other end of the curtain rail.'

'It isn't funny,' said James. But he started to laugh as well.

'Come on,' said Mandy at last. 'Let's try a two-pronged attack.'

They got two chairs set up in front of the curtains and at last managed to trap the hamster between them. Mandy made a final lunge and got it. 'There,' she said, putting it with the others. 'And don't open that cage again,' she said to Tommy.

Mandy and James watched the little boy trot off down the path. Walter Pickard was waiting at the bottom of the lane. He waved to them as Tommy ran towards him.

'They must be going to the show,' said James.

'And at least *we* can get to the show now,' said Mandy.

But just then the phone rang. Mandy picked it up and spoke for a few moments, then she put the receiver down and turned a worried face to James.

'What is it?' he said.

'That was Dad,' she said. 'He's had an urgent call to one of the farms up on the moor.'

James was puzzled. 'It isn't anything terrible, is it?'

Mandy shook her head. 'No,' she said. 'It isn't that I'm worried about — it's Prince.'

'Prince?' said James.

'Dad was going to look at him — check him over. I knew Dad wouldn't let him jump if he wasn't fit. But Prince and Susan haven't arrived yet and Dad had to go. So now there won't be anybody to check Prince out.' Her heart was beating double time.

'You're worried, aren't you?' said James.

Mandy nodded. 'I am *now*,' she said. 'I was depending on Dad being able to see him before the competition.' She bit her lip. 'This morning Mum said it might be an allergy and allergies can be dangerous. I just know Susan is going to ride Prince flat out. She says she's going to win whatever happens.'

Mandy looked at James. 'We've got to find out what's wrong with Prince, James. We've got to do something!'

Ten

They pedalled as fast as they could. Mandy had popped Toby into her bicycle basket. The puppy seemed to enjoy the ride. Blackie ran along at James's side. Soon the village church was in sight — and Farmer Redpath's field behind.

They swerved through the church gate and left their bikes propped against the porch. Mandy tucked Toby under her arm and they ran round to the low wall at the back of the church and hopped over. It was quicker than going through the gate. At once they were in the middle of the tents and stalls and marquees.

In the distance Mandy caught a glimpse of Duke. the shire horse all decked out in brasses and ribbons. People called out to her and James, but they didn't stop. She wanted to get to the jumping ring as quickly as possible. She didn't even stop when Jean waved to them from behind the cake and candy stall. Mandy just waved back and kept on running, nearly knocking over the cake display at the cake competition stand.

Mrs Ponsonby came out from the far end of the cake display stand and tutted. She was wearing an enormous pink hat with feathers in it. Pandora, as usual, was under her arm.

'Sorry, Mrs Ponsonby,' Mandy muttered.

'Sorry isn't good enough,' said Mrs Ponsonby. 'You should be more careful, young lady,' and she stood right in front of Mandy beside the biggest chocolate cake on the stand.

'Sorry,' said Mandy again. Toby tried to squirm out of her grasp to make friends with Pandora. Pandora yipped a greeting to Toby. Mrs Ponsonby gave the puppy a sideways look and shifted Pandora to her other arm. Pandora suddenly became very quiet. Mandy stole a look at her and started to say, 'Mrs Pon—'

But Mrs Ponsonby was in full flood. Mandy and

James got a complete lecture on the manners of the younger generation, society today and the dangers of running when you should walk. Finally Mandy could bear it no longer. 'Mrs Ponsonby,' she said loudly. 'Pandora is eating that chocolate cake.'

Mrs Ponsonby turned in horror. Pandora, still in her arms, was making her way steadily through the cake. 'My cake!' screeched Mrs Ponsonby. 'My beautiful cake!' She turned to Mandy. 'This is your fault,' she said.

Mandy could control her temper no longer. 'It isn't my fault,' she snapped. 'If you didn't give that poor little dog chocolates to eat all the time she would know better. You have to train dogs. It's for their own good. Poor Pandora can hardly walk, she's so fat. It's not my fault, Mrs Ponsonby. It's yours!'

Mrs Ponsonby was so angry she couldn't speak. Even the feathers on her hat trembled in rage. Blackie barked and looked longingly at them. James grabbed his collar with one hand and Mandy's arm with the other. 'Come on,' he whispered in Mandy's ear. 'Let's get out of here — quick.'

They left Mrs Ponsonby still staring after them, speechless.

Then they were at the jumping ring. Mandy looked round. No sign of Susan. Then she caught sight of the blue Jaguar with the horse box in tow. A pretty fair-haired woman in a flower patterned dress got out of the car. Mandy recognised her from television. It was Susan's mum.

A few people turned and spotted her. All at once she was surrounded by people with bits of paper. She began signing autographs.

Susan got out of the back of the car and caught Mandy's eye. 'Look,' she seemed to say. 'Look what a famous mother I have.'

Susan looked terrific. Her hair was tucked up under the riding-hat and her boots were polished to a high shine. She went round to the back of the horse box and began to undo the ramp.

Mandy's eyes fastened on Prince as he stepped daintily down the ramp. She was a bit far away to tell but she thought he looked winded. But how could he be winded? He had only just arrived.

'What are you going to do?' asked James.

'Try talking to Susan,' said Mandy, 'but I don't think she'll listen.'

They made their way over to the horse box. Mandy looked at Prince. His sides were heaving and he coughed. She took a deep breath. 'I don't think you should jump Prince,' she said.

Susan's head came up. 'What?' she said.

Mandy bit her lip. 'I don't think he's well enough. Look at him. He's out of breath.'

Susan's eyes hardened. 'You just don't want me to win,' she said.

'That isn't true,' Mandy protested. But Susan wasn't listening.

'Just wait,' Susan said. 'You'll see what Prince can do.' She looked at Mandy. 'I've told you it's just a cold. I kept him warm and dry in his stable all day yesterday. He'll be fine. He just needs a bit of exercise. And if you think I'm going to give up without even trying to win you're mistaken.' Susan's face suddenly lit up. 'Don't you realise?' she said. 'If I win Mum is going to be so proud. She might even come and live with us here.'

It took a moment for it to sink in. So that was why Susan was so determined to win. It wasn't just the winning after all. Mandy's mind was in a whirl.

Susan looked at her and her face softened. 'Look,' she said almost kindly, 'I must go and see Mum. You take care of Prince for me. We aren't on until the third group.'

Mandy watched her run off across the field. She put Toby down on the grass, turned to Prince and laid her head against his neck. It felt damp but his breathing had quietened a little.

'How is he?' said James.

Mandy turned to him. 'I don't know,' she said. 'I wish Dad was here.'

James's mouth set. 'I'll go and see if he's back yet,' he said, running off.

Mandy watched him go. She didn't think her father would be back yet. And she knew now that there was no way Susan would give up a chance of winning — she wouldn't let herself believe there was anything wrong with Prince. She wanted so much to win — to impress her mother.

But it wasn't 'just a cold'. Susan had been fooling herself. Prince was really ill and if Susan wasn't going to do anything about it then Mandy would have to.

Just then a race steward passed by. Mandy stopped him. 'I don't think this pony is fit to jump,' she said.

He looked at her. 'Is he your pony?'

Mandy shook her head. 'No, but I think he's unwell.'

The steward ran a hand over the pony's legs and flanks. 'I can't see anything wrong with him. Why don't you take him over to the vet?'

For a moment Mandy's spirits rose. 'Is he back?'

James appeared at her elbow. 'No luck,' he said. 'He still isn't here.'

Mandy looked at the race steward. The man spread his hands. 'There's nothing I can do,' he said. 'The pony doesn't belong to you and I'm not a vet.' He gave Prince another look. 'Anyway, he looks all right to me,' he said.

Mandy watched him walk away. She was in despair. She tried to think, but there was so little time. Already the Tannoy was announcing the pony trials, asking the first group of riders and mounts to assemble. She could see Barry Prescott on his bay gelding, trotting him, warming him up. And Susan was going to try and beat a strong horse like that.

Mandy began to walk Prince over the grass towards the jumping ring. The air blew fresh and a cool little breeze sprang up. She laid her hand on Prince's flank. His breathing was easier now — hardly noticeable and he had stopped coughing.

'How's the little fellow?' said a voice behind her.

It was Grandad. He gave Prince a pat. 'We miss him, your gran and I,' he said. 'We used to like popping along to see him in that little lean-to.' He scratched his head. 'That reminds me,' he said. 'I must go and make sure that Duke is well away from those hay bales. Don't want him coming down with the heaves. Not that they call it that these days. Got some fancy name for it now. But it doesn't matter what they call it — it could still do for old Duke.'

'Do for him?' said Mandy.

Grandad looked at her. 'That time when Duke got locked in the hay barn. He collapsed — nearly died. Luckily Dan got him out in time. It would have broken Dan's heart if Duke had died.' And he strode off across the field.

Mandy watched him for a moment, her mind beginning to work overtime, putting things together. She looked over to where the horse box stood empty. Wisps of hay blew about inside it. She turned and looked at the jumping ring, at the jump Prince had refused — the hay bales. She thought of Prince's stable and how warm and dry it was. Dusty dry — dust from the straw on the floor and the haynet. He had been in there all day yesterday.

'What is it?' said James.

Mandy turned a worried face to him. 'They have got a fancy name for it now,' she said. 'It's called SAD, only I can't remember what that stands for. Mum was talking about it the other day.' She clutched James's arm. 'James, I'm nearly sure that's what's wrong with Prince. His stable is dusty with hay, not like his old stable. He wheezes when he's been shut up in the horse box and he refused the hay bales jump. I think Mum was right. I think he *is* allergic — to hay.'

The Tannoy burst into life again and the first rider started off round the course. Mandy watched. One fence cleared, the next down, two more cleared then the hay bales. As the pony's hooves touched the top of the jump, wisps of hay flew up. By the time it was Prince's turn there would be hay blowing about everywhere.

She looked across the field. Susan was standing in a group with Mrs Ponsonby, Gran and Mr Hadcroft the vicar — and her mother. They were having their photos taken.

Maybe Mandy was wrong. Just because the shire horse had an allergy didn't mean Prince had it. Then the last piece of the jigsaw fitted into place. Grandad had been looking at Prince when he remembered Duke. Prince had reminded him of Duke. Why? The answer came to her loud and clear: because they both hated hay.

She looked at Prince. He was breathing easily. He looked as fit as could be. But what if he jumped? Mandy couldn't bear to think about what might happen. She thought of the panic and fear in Prince's eyes as he cleared the hay bale jump. How much worse would that be today? Duke had nearly died from the heaves. Mandy couldn't let that happen to Prince.

She turned to James, her mind made up. 'Will you help me?' she said.

James looked puzzled. 'Help you to do what?' he said. 'You heard the steward. There's nothing we can do.'

Mandy's mouth set in a grim line. 'Oh, yes, there is,' she said.

James looked even more puzzled. 'What?'

Mandy's head came up. 'We can steal Prince,' she said. 'Steal him and hide him until the jumping is over or until Dad gets here.'

The loudspeaker announced that the second group of ponies were to assemble. 'Steal him?' James said in a whisper.

Mandy nodded. 'Well? What about it? Are you with me?'

Eleven

James's face was a picture of concern.

'Steal Prince?' he said again.

Mandy nodded. 'To protect him. It's the only way.'

'We'll get into terrible trouble,' said James.

'Prince could get into worse trouble,' said Mandy. 'What if he collapsed on the course? What if he died? Grandad says Duke nearly did. And Susan is determined to make Prince jump.'

James took a deep breath. 'OK, I'm with you,' he said. 'What do we do?'

Mandy heaved a sigh of relief. She laid her hand

gently on Prince's neck. 'The first thing to do is decide where we're going to take him,' she said.

'But how are we going to get him away without somebody noticing?' James said.

Mandy bit her lip in concentration. 'You'll have to distract everybody's attention,' she said. 'Then I can slip Prince out of the show ring when everyone's looking the other way.'

'And how do I do that?' said James.

Mandy grinned. It was amazing how things fell into place when you were really determined. 'Blackie,' she said. 'You know how much he likes feathers.'

James looked at her. 'Are you thinking what I think you're thinking?' he said.

'Mrs Ponsonby's hat,' said Mandy.

James let out a whistle. 'After that stuff with the cake and Pandora she'll skin us alive.'

'But you'll do it?' said Mandy.

James nodded.

'OK,' she said. 'You get going. I'll try to look as if I'm just walking Prince, giving him a bit of exercise.'

'Wait a minute,' James said. 'Where are you going to take him?'

Mandy looked around the open field. There were no hiding places and if she tried to get him back to

Animal Ark she would be seen. Susan would be looking for Prince soon and James couldn't keep everyone's attention for ever, not even with the help of Blackie.

Then her eyes lit on the perfect hiding place. 'In there,' she said. 'In the church.'

'The *church*?' said James. 'What on earth will Mr Walters say?'

Mandy shook her head. 'I don't care,' she said. 'I just don't want Prince to have to jump. As long as I can keep him hidden until it's over, that's all I care about.'

'Right,' said James. 'You start walking him across and I'll get Blackie to do his stuff.'

Prince turned his head and blew softly on Mandy's cheek. She reached a hand up and laid her ear against his chest. Deep inside she could hear his breath. It sounded normal but if she was right, that didn't mean a thing. It was only when he was near hay that he couldn't breathe properly.

'It's all right, boy,' she said to him. 'You aren't going to jump until Dad's seen you — no matter what.'

The pony nuzzled her shoulder as if he understood. She began to walk him away from the jumping ring. James was running for the cake competition stand, Blackie at his heels and Toby trying to keep up. Susan had turned round. She was looking for Prince. Mandy urged Prince along. If she could get behind the belt of trees that fringed the churchyard she would have more chance of avoiding notice, but there was still a long way to go.

'Oh, James,' she muttered to herself. 'Hurry!'

Mandy could see Susan quite clearly. She was looking all around. Any moment now she would spot them and the game would be up. The loudspeaker crackled into life, announcing the start of the third group. Susan began to look more urgently.

'Oh, please hurry, James,' Mandy muttered.

Then from the other side of the field came a long-drawn-out howling. Something large and black shot across the jumping ring and began to caper madly. Blackie! Mrs Ponsonby's hat was firmly clasped between his teeth. A figure ran after it — James. He was closely followed by several others. In moments the ring was covered with people all trying to catch the Labrador. Blackie was turning and twisting, keeping one step ahead of everyone chasing him.

Mandy risked another glance at Susan. Her dad was there now. She and her parents had turned towards the commotion.

'*Now*,' Mandy said to Prince, and she urged the

little pony across the open space to the belt of trees. Sounds rose in the air behind her but she ignored them. They were coming from the show ring. No one was looking in her direction.

As swiftly as she could she urged the pony on. She didn't want to hurry him too much but they didn't have much time.

'Not far now, Prince,' she whispered.

Behind them the loudspeaker began to bellow to people to clear the ring. And then the church was there — only metres away.

Mandy gave one more glance backwards and drew Prince across the open space to the door. She laid a hand on the heavy handle of the door into the church porch, hoping that it would be open. For a moment she thought it was locked and her heart sank. Then the heavy ring turned in her hand and the door opened. Mandy urged Prince through into the cool dimness of the porch.

She closed the door behind them, then she went and laid a hand on Prince's flank. 'There, boy,' she said. 'You're safe now. And you aren't going back — not until the jumping is over.

Prince whickered and nuzzled Mandy's shoulder. She turned her face into his warm neck and laid her hand on his mane. 'It's all right, Prince,' she whispered. 'Dad will be here soon. He'll know what to do.'

She stroked a hand across his coat and felt his sides heave slightly under her fingers. He was sweating a little. But she had led him gently enough towards the church — or as gently as she had been able. His eyes seemed to be pleading with her, asking for help.

Mandy loosened his girth and took off his saddle. She looked round. She needed something to rub him down with. He was cooling rapidly now.

But the porch was empty. She tried the door into the church. Locked. Then she saw a cupboard in the corner. She tugged the door open. Buckets, brooms and — dusters. They looked clean enough.

Quickly Mandy wadded up a pile of dusters and began to rub Prince down, talking to him all the while — soothing him, making small reassuring noises. After a while she could feel him grow calmer. She worked on and on until he was warm. She breathed a sigh of relief. If she could just keep him here until Dad came back from Twyford. If she could let him rest . . .

There was a sound at the porch door and a grating noise as it opened. Mandy froze. She looked round wildly but there was nowhere else to hide. She put herself between the door and Prince.

A shadow fell across the floor of the porch as the door opened. James poked his head inside. Mandy felt her breath come out in a great rush of relief.

'Oh, James, you did a terrific job. Thanks a lot.'

'I thought you might need help.' James said. He rested his hand on Prince's neck. 'How is he?' he said.

Mandy shook her head. 'He seems better now but even a little exercise seems to distress him. What's happening outside?' she said. 'Where's Susan?'

James's face fell. 'She knows, Mandy. She says you've taken her pony. She told the race steward and they're looking for you. It's only a matter of time before they find us.'

'They'll never look here,' said Mandy. 'They'd never think of looking for a pony in a church porch.'

James didn't seem too sure. 'Once they've looked everywhere else,' he said. 'I mean, where else is there to look?'

Mandy thought for a moment. 'What about you?' she said to James. 'Did anybody see you come this way?'

James shook his head. 'Nobody was bothered about me,' he said. 'Not once I'd caught Blackie and made him give Mrs Ponsonby her hat back. By that time Susan had everybody looking for the pony.'

'You're sure no one saw you?' said Mandy.

James shook his head. 'Positive,' he said.

Just then there came a scratching at the porch door.

Mandy jumped. 'What's that?' she said.

James went red. 'Oh, no!' he said.

He went to the door and opened it. Blackie bounded in. In his mouth he·was carrying Mrs Ponsonby's hat.

James groaned. 'Oh, no, Blackie,' he said. 'You didn't steal it again . . .' Then his voice trailed off.

'What is it?' Mandy said.

James was looking towards Farmer Redpath's field. Mandy came to stand beside him. There was a small stream of people heading their way. Mrs Ponsonby was among them. And at that moment Susan looked up — and saw Mandy. Susan turned to her father and pointed. Quickly Mandy hid behind the porch door but she knew it was too late. Susan had seen her.

She looked at James. 'She's coming, isn't she?' she said.

James nodded and turned to Mandy. 'It looks like we're in an awful lot of trouble,' he said.

Twelve

Mandy put her arm round Prince's neck, as if to protect him.

'We could make a run for it,' said James.

Mandy shook her head. 'That's just the point,' she said. 'We can't. We're here to stop Prince running. I couldn't do that to him.'

James looked miserable. 'So what do we do when they come?'

Mandy's shoulders slumped. 'Try to convince them there's something wrong with Prince,' she said. 'But they'll never believe me. Nobody believes me.' There were tears in her eyes.

'I believe you,' said James.

Blackie whined gently and came and laid Mrs Ponsonby's hat at Mandy's feet. Even though she felt so terrible she couldn't help smiling.

'And Blackie believes you,' said James.

Just then the porch door burst open and a crowd of people poured in. Toby was with them.

Everyone started shouting at once. Mandy could hardly think for the noise. Above all came the voice of Mrs Ponsonby. 'My hat!' she cried. 'Look at my poor hat.'

Mandy looked down at the crushed bundle of pink felt and feathers.

Then Susan said, 'I told you she had taken Prince.'

Mandy's head came up. 'He isn't well,' she said. 'There's something wrong with him.'

'Do you realise what you've done?' the race steward said angrily to Mandy.

Mandy took a deep breath. 'Prince isn't fit to jump,' she said.

The race steward looked at her, then at Prince. 'I've already told you. He seems all right to me,' he said.

'He's all right now,' said Mandy 'but—'

She didn't get any further. 'Why are we wasting

time?' Susan said to her father. 'You can see for yourself Prince is OK.'

Mandy felt desperate. 'There is something wrong with Prince,' she said. 'I know it.'

'What?' said the race steward.

Suddenly Mandy felt her confidence draining away. What if she was wrong after all? But she couldn't take the risk. 'I think it's SAD,' she said loudly.

'It certainly is sad when a young woman behaves the way you have,' said Mrs Ponsonby.

'I didn't mean that,' said Mandy.

'What did you mean then?' said the race steward.

Mandy drew herself up. 'It's an illness called SAD. It's like asthma in people. The heaves. I think he's allergic to hay.'

'That's three diseases already,' said Mrs Ponsonby.

The race steward looked exasperated. 'You stole a pony,' he said. 'That's a pretty serious thing to do.'

'It's serious for Prince,' she said. 'If you let him jump and he gets hay in his lungs he might die — if I'm right about this.'

'*If* you're right,' said Mrs Ponsonby. 'So you admit you might be wrong, do you? That's a change.'

'If you'd only listen . . .' said Mandy. She looked round helplessly. Her eyes came to rest on Susan's father. He was the only one who hadn't said anything yet. He had a kind face — and he didn't look angry, just puzzled.

'I don't know anything about horses,' he said, 'but if there's any doubt about the pony's health maybe we should get a vet to look at him.'

'Her dad is a vet,' said Susan. 'So is her mum. That's why she thinks she knows it all.'

Mrs Ponsonby cut in. 'She *does* think she knows it all,' she said. 'Why she even told me how to look after my little Pandora.'

'You aren't feeding her properly,' Mandy shouted, unable to stop herself. It was the wrong thing to say.

'What did I tell you?' Mrs Ponsonby said, turning to Susan's father. 'Cheeky little madam. Interfering with people and their pets. How can you believe a little vandal like that? Standing there bold as brass with my hat.' And she reached over and snatched up her hat.

Mandy looked at Mr Collins. He was her last hope. But she knew she had lost.

'The pony looks all right to me,' he said.

Mandy tried one last time. 'He *looks* all right,' she

said, 'but he isn't. I'm sure he isn't.'

The race steward looked at his watch again. 'Make up your mind,' he said.

'If you could give us proof . . .' said Mr Collins.

Mandy shook her head. 'I haven't got any proof,' she said miserably.

The race steward opened the porch door. 'What's it to be then?' he said,

Mr Collins took hold of Prince's bridle as Susan began to buckle on the saddle. 'I'm sure your intentions were good,' he said. 'But if the race steward doesn't see anything wrong with Prince . . .' He hesitated, 'Besides, his previous owners said the pony had always been healthy.'

'That's just it,' Mandy said. 'It's his feeding and his stabling. It's all wrong. The stables where he lived before—'

She didn't get any further. Mr Collins interrupted her. 'Mrs Jackson was delighted with the stables at The Beeches,' he said.

'They're brand new,' said Susan. 'Poor Prince was living in a lean-to before we bought him.'

'But it was healthier for him.' Mandy protested.

At that Mrs Ponsonby drew herself up. 'Really, it's too much,' she said to Mr Collins. 'First I don't know how to feed a dog, then you don't know how to stable a horse. I won't listen to another word of this nonsense. A lean-to healthier than a proper stable? It's ridiculous.' She looked round. 'I suppose you would keep a pony in a porch,' she said to Mandy.

It was the worst moment of Mandy's life. She watched dumbly as Susan led Prince out of the porch. The others walked on ahead. At the last moment Susan turned back. 'You think I don't love Prince as much as you do,' she said. 'but I do — and I'm going to win with him because he's just the best pony in the world.'

Mandy stood there dumbly as they disappeared. Even Toby went with them. She had tried her best. Tried — and failed.

Mandy and James stood outside the church porch watching the small procession heading towards the ring. The loudspeaker announced that Barry Prescott had a clear round. Mandy's heart turned over. That meant Susan had to win on time alone. A clear round wouldn't be enough. She would have to push Prince to the limit.

'Oh, I wish Dad would come,' Mandy said. 'I keep thinking about Duke nearly dying. And he's a big strong shire horse.'

'Do you really think that might happen to Prince?'

said James. 'Do you think he might collapse?'

Mandy nodded. 'Even walking him this far made him breathless. And if he gets hay in his lungs from the jump—' Mandy stopped. She couldn't bear to think of it.

James nodded. 'What's that?'

Mandy turned her head to the road behind them. A Land-rover was coming down the road towards the church, making for the turning into Farmer Redpath's field. She looked towards the jumping ring. Susan was up on Prince, trotting him round the field, ready to go into the ring. She looked back towards the road. She could see the car more clearly now. She grabbed James's sleeve. 'It's Dad,' she said. 'Stop him. Get him to come at once to the ring. I don't care what he says. Just get him there.'

And then she was halfway down the path, running.

James's eyes were wide. 'Where are you going?' he yelled.

Mandy turned as she ran. 'To stop Prince jumping,' she called back. 'Get Dad — I'll hold them up as long as I can.'

As she ran she risked one last look back. James was on his way, flying towards the turning to stop the Land-rover. Blackie was like a shadow at his heels. She hoped he would make it — hoped he would be able to persuade her father that it was a matter of life or death.

Her feet pounded on the path. The breath rasped in her throat but she paid no attention. Her eyes were fixed on the ring. She saw Susan bring Prince up to the start, waiting for the signal to begin her round.

Mandy reached the belt of trees and crashed through them, not caring about the scratches she got from branches. She was nearly there. Only a few more metres to go.

Susan had started her canter round the ring, then she would start the jumps. Mandy increased her pace. Suddenly she felt her foot catch in a tree root. She went over, tumbling heavily to the ground. The impact of her fall drove the breath out of her body.

She struggled up and made to run again. There was a searing pain in her ankle and she felt weak in her stomach. She looked towards the ring. Susan was gathering the reins, urging Prince into a gallop.

Mandy tested the weight on her left foot. It was agony. She gritted her teeth. Running, hobbling, ignoring the pain, she made her way through the rest of the trees and into the ring. All she could think of was Prince. He mustn't gallop. She repeated it to herself, trying to blot out the pain in her foot. *He mustn't gallop. He mustn't jump.* She was running down the middle of the ring now, running straight for Prince.

'Stop!' she cried. 'You must stop!'

Mandy could see the race steward running out on to the field. She could see the faces of the other riders looking at her in shock. She could see Susan's face turned to her in disbelief.

She made one last effort. The pain in her foot was almost blinding her now. Gathering her strength, she ran on past the five-bar gate, past the hay bales. Prince recognised her and threw his head up, whickering. Susan let the reins drop and he slowed, breathing heavily. Mandy saw the double line of his breath heave through his flanks.

She reached him and threw an arm round his neck. Susan looked down at her. 'What are you doing?' she said angrily. 'You've ruined everything.'

Mandy could hardly speak. She was so out of breath and the pain in her foot was coming in waves now. Around her people had started to gather, people shouting, asking questions, demanding what she was up to. Some of the riders had dismounted and were coming towards her, leading their ponies.

But she had stopped Susan and Prince! Mandy didn't care what they would do to her. She didn't care that they were shouting at her. She only cared

about Prince. He wouldn't have to jump now.

The race steward stood in front of her, his face red with anger. 'This is going too far . . .' he began.

Mandy leaned against Prince for support, trying to gather her strength.

Then another voice spoke, a voice she knew and trusted. 'What's the trouble?' said Mr Hope. 'Mandy? Are you all right?'

Mandy turned to her father in relief. James was beside him, grinning. 'You did it, Mandy!' he said.

Mandy managed a smile before she said to her father, 'It's Prince, Dad, you mustn't let him jump.'

And then, in front of them all, she slid down the pony's flank and fainted.

Thirteen

'We'll have to issue tickets soon, you're getting so many visitors,' Mr Hope joked.

Mandy looked up at him. It was the Thursday after the Welford Show and she was sitting in a deckchair in the sunny garden behind Animal Ark, her leg propped up on a stool. Her foot was still swathed in a crepe bandage but the swelling wasn't nearly so bad now.

'Hello, Mr Pickard,' she said as Walter came up the path. Tommy was with him, holding his cage of hamsters. 'Not more chewing-gum, Tommy?' she said.

Tommy blushed. 'I brought them to see you,' he said, holding out the cage. 'They won a prize at the show.'

'The prize for the most unusual appearance,' said Mr Hope. 'I donated the prize myself.'

Walter chuckled but Tommy was clearly proud of his prize. 'It was a jumbo pack of chewing-gum,' he said. 'Just for me.'

Mandy looked at the little animals. They still looked a bit odd but their fur was beginning to grow back.

'How's the invalid?' said Walter.

Mandy smiled. 'I'm fine,' she said. 'But people are making a terrible fuss of me.'

'We can't move for get well cards and the house has more flowers in it than the garden does,' said Mr Hope.

This time it was Mandy's turn to blush. She hadn't realised how popular she was. Every day had brought more visitors.

On Sunday it had been Kate and Melanie. 'A week off school,' Melanie said. 'Lucky you!'

'She nearly had to break her ankle for it,' Kate said. 'I didn't know you hated school that much, Mandy.'

Mandy smiled at the thought as she played with

Tommy's hamsters while Dad and Walter had a talk about Mum's roses and Tommy went into the house for some lemonade. Her ankle hadn't been broken — just very badly sprained.

'You were lucky there,' Dr Prescott had said. 'But you'll have to keep it up for a week.'

'Try some of your dad's liniment,' Barry had said when he came on Monday. 'It worked like magic for Star.' Mandy nearly took him seriously till she saw the glint in his eyes. 'Anyway,' he said, 'I thought what you did was marvellous.'

Mandy tickled one of the hamsters under the chin and remembered how she had come out of that faint and had looked at Prince safe in Dad's care. She would gladly have broken an ankle for Prince's sake.

Then there was Gran and Grandad and the McFarlanes and Betty Hilder and the Mabsons and Penny Hapwell and her mum with Cally and the Metcalfs and Mr Hardy — the list was endless. Even Dan Venables came to see her.

'You saved that pony's life, I reckon,' he said when Mrs Hope brought him in.

Mandy had looked at him in alarm. 'Was it really as bad as that?'

Dan looked at Mrs Hope. 'You'd have to ask the expert,' he said. 'But I reckon you did.'

'There was a lot of dust in Prince's airways,' said Mrs Hope. 'Hay dust mostly but fine sawdust as well and mould spores from his bedding. If he had been forced to jump there's no telling what might have happened. He had been in that stable all day Friday. He was pretty weak in the chest by Saturday. If he had been pushed too hard he could have been harmed for life.'

'So I did the right thing, Mum?' said Mandy.

Mrs Hope nodded. 'Oh, yes, Mandy, you did the right thing. Everybody knows that now.'

Two of the nicest visitors were Jane and Mrs Jackson.

'Prince never had any trouble with his chest when we owned him,' Mrs Jackson said.

'That's because we kept him in the open most of the time, Mum,' Jane said. 'And we fed him lots of oats and bran and let him graze in the orchard.'

'Dad always said there wasn't a better looked after pony in the district,' said Mandy.

'He'll be all right now, won't he?' said Mrs Jackson. 'If they aren't looking after him properly I'll go right over there and bring him home.'

Mandy laughed. Little Mrs Jackson looked so fierce. 'You don't have to do that,' she said. 'Dad has seen to all that. He says Susan has a bedroom full of books on how to look after ponies now — and her mum is helping her.'

That was another thing. Susan's mum hadn't gone back to London straightaway. She had stayed on at The Beeches.

'Susan says her mum and dad are talking about her mum doing less TV work and spending more time up here,' James said on one of his daily visits.

Mandy bit her lip. 'Susan hasn't come to see me,' she said. 'I mean her mum and dad sent this great big basket of flowers . . .'

'She's too embarrassed,' James said. 'She says she can't face you, she feels so awful.'

Mandy looked up, surprised. 'That's daft,' she said. 'How was she to know? She doesn't know anything about horses — apart from how to ride them.'

'She's trying to learn,' James said.

Mandy grew thoughtful. Maybe Susan was changing. Then she thought of something else. 'James,' she said. 'What has happened to Toby?'

James shuffled. 'He's got a new home,' he said. 'He's really happy there.' James sounded surprised.

'That's what Mum and Dad say,' said Mandy. 'But they won't tell me where he is.'

'I'd better go,' said James. And Mandy just knew he was hiding something from her.

But now it was Thursday and Susan still hadn't come to see her. Mandy dozed in the deckchair. The sun was warm and she felt her eyes closing. Vaguely she heard sounds. A kind of *clip-clop*, like a pony coming up the path.

Her eyes flew open. It was a pony. It was Prince — and he looked wonderful. His coat gleamed, his eyes were bright and he whinnied and tried to pull away from Susan.

Susan let the leading-rein go and Prince made his way delicately across the grass, bent his head and nuzzled Mandy's ear. He blew gently and her hair lifted. 'That tickles,' she said to him reaching up to stroke his nose. 'Oh, Prince, I'm so glad to see you.'

'He's all right now,' said Susan. 'He really is. Your dad says so.'

Mandy looked at Susan standing there, awkward, near to tears. 'I'm so sorry, Mandy,' she said. 'I should have listened to you. I nearly killed Prince. I don't know what to say.'

Mandy smiled. 'Everything is OK now,' she said and saw Susan's shoulders sag with relief.

'And you'll help me to look after him?' said Susan.

Mandy laughed. 'Just try to keep me away,' she said.

Behind Susan she could see Mr and Mrs Collins coming up the path. Prince moved away and began to crop the short grass of the lawn.

'We might have to get another horse soon,' said Susan's dad, smiling at his wife.

'If I can get away more often,' Mrs Collins said. 'I'm going to try and cut down on work a bit.'

'And so am I,' said Mr Collins. 'Susan will soon be complaining that she can't get rid of us.'

But when Mandy looked at Susan's happy face she didn't think that would be a problem. Susan looked really content — and much more at home. Mandy thought she might have found a new friend.

The garden gate swung open again just as Mandy's parents came out of the house. It was James and Blackie and behind them was someone else: Mrs Ponsonby. But something was different. She was still wearing the pink hat. It was a bit bashed but it still had its feathers.

For a moment Mandy couldn't work out what had changed. Then she realised Mrs Ponsonby wasn't carrying Pandora. Mandy looked down. There was Pandora waddling up the path and by her side — Toby!

'See why we didn't tell you before,' Mr Hope said to Mandy. 'Mrs Ponsonby decided to adopt him. We didn't think you'd be able to stand the shock.'

Mrs Ponsonby sailed up the path. In her hands she carried an enormous box of chocolates tied up with a yellow ribbon. 'My dear brave child,' she said, 'what you did was a lesson to us all. Risking yourself for that sweet little pony as you did. Such courage. I was saying to your grandmother only today how proud she must be of you.'

Mandy just gaped while Mrs Ponsonby went on about her being an example to other young people. Pandora and Toby played happily at her feet.

Pandora even managed a little run — almost. Was it Mandy's imagination or had Pandora slimmed down a bit?

Blackie came and plonked himself down beside Mandy and started licking her face. Then Mrs Ponsonby presented the chocolates to her with a flourish and bent to kiss her cheek. If it hadn't been for her ankle Mandy would have tried to run away. As it was she had to grab Blackie's collar as the feathers came within reach.

'Don't eat them all at once,' Mrs Ponsonby said, straightening up. 'After all too many chocolates aren't good for you. I don't give my precious Pandora or Toby anything like that. Aren't they wonderful together? They have such fun and Pandora really is becoming quite lively.'

Mandy looked around. The garden was full to bursting with people and animals. Mum and Dad, Susan and her parents, James, Mrs Ponsonby, Blackie and Toby and Pandora. There was one animal missing, though. 'Where's Prince?' she said.

James's eyes opened wide. 'In the porch,' he said, 'eating the geraniums.'

'Oh, that's all right then,' said Mandy.

'Is it?' said Mr Collins. 'I mean — the porch?'

Mrs Ponsonby turned to him majestically. 'Mr

Collins,' she said, 'if Mandy says a pony in the porch
is all right, then a pony in the porch is all right.'

And then everybody laughed — even Mrs
Ponsonby.

ANIMAL ARK *by Lucy Daniels*

All Hodder Children's books are available at your local bookshop, or can be ordered direct from the publisher. Just tick the titles you would like and complete the details below. Prices and availability are subject to change without prior notice.

Please enclose a cheque or postal order made payable to *Bookpoint Ltd*, and send to: Hodder Children's Books, 39 Milton Park, Abingdon, OXON, OX14 4TD, UK. Email Address: orders@bookpoint.co.uk

If you would prefer to pay by credit card, our call centre team would be delighted to take your order by telephone. Our direct line *01235 400414* (lines open 9.00 am – 6.00 pm Monday to Saturday, 24 hour message answering service). Alternatively you can send a fax on *01235 400454*.

TITLE		FIRST NAME		SURNAME	

ADDRESS	
DAYTIME TEL:		POST CODE	

If you would prefer to pay by credit card, please complete: Please debit my Visa/Access/Diner's Card/American Express (delete as applicable) card no:

☐☐☐☐ ☐☐☐☐ ☐☐☐☐ ☐☐☐☐

Signature ....

Expiry Date: ....

If you would NOT like to receive further information on our products please tick the box. ☐

ANIMAL ACTION

If you like *Animal Ark* then you'll love the RSPCA's Animal Action Club! Anyone aged 13 or under can become a member for just £5.50 a year. Join up and you can look forward to six issues of Animal Action magazine - each one is bursting with animal news, competitions, features, posters and celebrity interviews. Plus we'll send you a fantastic joining pack too!

To be really animal-friendly just complete the form – a photocopy is fine – and send it, with a cheque or postal order for £5.50

(made payable to the RSPCA), to Animal Action Club, RSPCA, Causeway, Horsham, West Sussex RH12 1HG. We'll then send you a joining pack and your first copy of *Animal Action.*

Registered charity no 219099

Don't delay, join today!

Name
....

Address
....

....

Postcode
....

Date of birth
....

Youth membership of the Royal Society for the Prevention of Cruelty to Animals

AACHOD2